BETWEEN THE MOON AND THE WALKING

An Excursion into Emotion and Art

John Ruskan

R. Wyler & Co.
New York, NY

BETWEEN THE MOON AND THE WALKING
by JOHN RUSKAN

Copyright © 2012 John Ruskan

No part of this book may be reproduced by any mechanical, photographic or electronic process, or in the form of a phonographic recording, nor may it be stored in a retrieval system, transmitted, translated into another language, or otherwise copied for public or private use without the permission of the publisher, excepting brief passages constituting "fair use," quoted for purposes of review.

The author of this book does not presume to offer psychological therapy nor advocate the use of any technique for the treatment of any specific or traumatic psychological condition without the approval and guidance of a qualified psychologist. The intent of the author is only to relate his personal experience in the hope that it may help you in your quest for emotional and spiritual health. If you use any of the information as a form of self-therapy, the author and publisher assume no responsibility for your actions.

ISBN: 9780962929519

Published by:
R. Wyler & Co.
147 West 22 St.
New York, NY
rwyler@emclear.com

Printed in the United States of America

cover by *Art Is*

dedicated to the
artist in all of us

special thanks for editing and
other invaluable assistance:
Charity Cygal, Steven Hirsch,
Tony Hoffman

This book endeavors to take the reader on an artistic and psychological journey into the collective unconscious while discussing how to make the most of the experience of art as a viewer. It's companion volume, *Emotion and Art*, explores the process of the artist in creating art.

Between the Moon and the Walking

EXCURSION **1**
BLUEGRASS 7
FLYING 9
LOFT 11
RUNNING 12
HIGHER ORDER 14
COINS 15
DENTISTRY 16
GEORGE 18
FLOWERS 19
SUBWAY 20
ENCOUNTER 21
FAST 24
SUPERMARKET 25
LAUNDRY 26
MAGIC **27**
PRESIDENT 33
MEN'S ROOM 35
THREE DREAMS 36
MARRIED 39
SMILE 40
ESCALATOR 41
NEWARK 42
BRAKES 44
SHIP 45
MOTORCYCLE 46
MIRROR 48
EUROPE 49
PAINTING 50
UNCONSCIOUS **53**
ICE 58
RECORDING 59
WAITING 62
FILM 64
KICK 65
LEADER 66
HIGHER 68
BOAT 69

ABOVE	70
ROAD	73
RESTAURANT	74
GRAVITY	75
RIFLEMAN	80
HYPNOSIS	81
SHADOW	**82**
CONSTRUCTION	90
ROYALTY	93
CAFÉ	94
FAT	96
PHILOSOPHER	98
COMMUNE	99
PHOTOGRAPHY	100
LOCKER ROOM	102
GAS	103
TWO 100'S	105
BREAKFAST	106
SENSITIVE	108
PROTECT	109
ARCHETYPES	**110**
BUS	116
WRONG	118
HALLWAY	119
PERFECT	120
OIL	121
SUICIDE CLUB	122
DUCKS	127
RELEASE	128
NATURAL HISTORY	130
ZOMBIE	131
TV	132
TALK	134
FIND OUT	136
REASON	138
NEXT LIFE	139
WRESTLING	140
MEETING	141
SERIOUS	142
MOON AND WALKING	**143**
PANTS	149
about JOHN	155

EXCURSION

My previous book, *Emotional Clearing*, described an approach for working with and releasing negative feelings trapped in the subconscious. In a way, writing that book was an attempt for me to finally organize my thoughts about how to work on myself, especially on troublesome feelings within me, an area generally neglected in the early training I had received on the spiritual path.

Writing and reading such a book is primarily an intellectual endeavor even though the discussion concerns feelings. But working on yourself usually requires getting into feelings and away from intellectualizations. It means opening to your feelings, which is not always as easy to do as it may sound. We retain our unconscious blocks and defenses to authentic, deep feeling – the same blocks that keep us from free-flowing artistic experience and expression. *Emotional Clearing* discusses these themes in depth, clarifying the nature of feelings and how we can move into a harmonious, beneficial relationship with our feeling selves.

As we move towards this harmonious relationship, we find that we enlarge our experience of ourselves and the world around us. Enlarging means, to a great extent, that we become aware of aspects of ourselves previously hidden. Many of these aspects are joyful, yielding pleasure and fulfillment as we grow into our higher-selves, such as the genuine capacity for love, but many are of a disturbing, dark nature. Some of this darkness may be attributed to parts of our primal, untamed lower-self that must be integrated into our growth. Many times, however, we meet with darkness from which we have unconsciously turned away, or suppressed, in the past. This is usually the case when we encounter events that trigger great emotion in us; the emotion is carried over from the past and projected onto the event. As you engage in any true and deep healing or consciousness work, you will come face to face with these painful, split-off, shadow parts of yourself. Confronting and resolving them with knowledge and courage is essential.

This present book continues with feelings work; however, rather than pursuing an intellectual dialogue, I've chosen to take a different, complementary approach, again sharing work that has been personally meaningful for me, but which is primarily feeling-oriented. Here, my objective is to communicate directly on the feeling level, intending that the material stimulate others into greater awareness, acceptance, experience, and transformation of their emotional selves.

In opening to this work, you will find deep, hidden feelings inside yourself activated. You will need to approach these feelings with care and concern, even with reverence, integrating them gently back into your conscious self. This is how art can be used on the path to wholeness – to bring us in touch with our forgotten selves, making it unnecessary for us to unconsciously project the negativity onto others as we are bound to do if we have no deliberate means of bringing it into awareness.

As I have assembled these stories, I have become acutely aware of the relationship between psychology and art. I would suggest these are two names for the same phenomena viewed from different angles. Psychology is the intellectual approach to the awareness of the inner self; art is the direct, feeling approach. We can make the most of our work on ourselves if we become conversant with both.

When we engage in the experience art offers, we enter the world of feeling, intuition, mystery, and healing – the world of the feminine. We must surrender to the power of this world and let it act on us. Those who resist the outer or inner feminine may have difficulty understanding what this work is about, and what art is about. Healing does not take place primarily as a result of understanding. We are realizing, although slowly, that growth and healing occur when we move from analysis to experience, from thinking to feeling. This is what we can learn to do most effectively in the arts. Involvement with the arts, either as observer or creator, serves to sensitize us to the world of feelings, increasing our "vocabulary" for feelings, developing the capacity for empathic communication.

To be empathic means to be able to put aside your own thoughts and feelings and to experience those of another. As this ability to go beyond self-centeredness grows, we find we deepen our relationship and identification with others, because in becoming sensitive to them, we are reminded of similar yet overlooked feelings inside ourselves. Extending the empathic capacity to ourselves means being able to quiet our surface thoughts and concerns, opening to the experience of ourselves, deeply, on the feeling level.

When we open to a piece of art, we must experience it empathically to get the greatest benefit from the interaction. In creating a work, the artist has instilled a certain feeling into it. The greater the work, the more authentic the feeling, and the more skillful the crafting of the form that contains the feeling. As we make intentional effort to still the mind, to take time to let the work affect us, as we visualize scenes, hear inner music, identify with personalities and circumstances described, and generally *feel* what it's like to be there from the inside, we open to the power of the art; we enter into the mystery of transformation. From within us are recalled those forgotten parts that resonate with the work. We journey to wholeness as we reclaim ourselves.

For art must remain a mystery to be felt, experienced, and lived through as we integrate and transcend the issues it re-presents. When we attempt to analyze art, to explain "what it means," we diminish its power, just as when we attempt to analyze ourselves.

The following stories have spontaneously emerged from visions, meditations, and dreams as I have traveled my path. They have been incredibly vivid for me, as if I have actually been there, in those circumstances, as real as my life on earth if not more so, but occurring in some other space of the psyche that has been called the astral plane. I always feel I am merely reporting and not inventing what I see, and that any attempt to "embellish" any piece results in a loss of power and truth.

The form the pieces have taken is unique: somewhere between poetry and short-story, in highly concentrated prose and sometimes free verse. I have found satisfaction in carefully crafting the language so it flows smoothly to my inner ear, trying to create a hypnotic effect to augment receptivity. I recommend you not try to read the stories at the same pace you would a novel; rather, linger with each story for as long as comfortable, possibly skipping randomly through the book. Let each story work on you as a kind of meditation, bringing you into a deeper place within yourself.

I always feel I am able to transcribe only a portion of the experience to paper, but this is where careful empathic reading can transport you not only fully into the places and spaces suggested, but to depths of your own that resonate with the descriptions. This is the path into the unknown, or more specifically, the subconscious, where we must journey to bring back to awareness the forgotten parts of ourselves. All true works of creation come from the unconscious, and most from the shadow aspect of the self – the forbidden, condemned qualities within that we have been conditioned to reject. This accounts for our fascination with such darkness as violence and sexual frustration.

The images presented here are not to be taken literally; they do not portray actual relationships or circumstances – it is the feeling behind them that is important. Moreover, they typically reflect a male point of view, are often self-centered, even sexist or racist; such is the uncensored content of the lower-self subconscious. I recognize they may be attacked by those who are unable to comprehend my intention or who are severely out of touch with their suppressed selves. But as these aspects of myself have spontaneously come forth, I have been fascinated by the depths they reflect, often with humor. It has become clear to me that by going deeply into the personal, I have reached into the archetypal collective – the feeling experiences common to us all. That is why the art of another can be so personally meaningful.

It seems we must go through the dark to reach the light, but we must not make the mistake of condemning the dark. Rather, we must learn to see our abhorrence of the dark as only a mind-set, a conditioning we must go beyond. As we befriend the darkness and those qualities we previously feared without acting them out, and learn how to constructively include them in our awareness and experience, we come more and more into wholeness and its intrinsic, transcendental joy. I wish you well.

BLUEGRASS

It's Sunday afternoon. I'm on the boardwalk at the Jersey shore. The boardwalk runs next to a busy street and is raised about six feet above it. On one of the corners of the street, where there are restaurants, motels, and such, a young woman starts to sing. Her words are hard to discern, but she attracts my attention and that of others. I am annoyed that she is stepping out of line by breaking an unspoken yet understood social code – she is not being quiet, she is not fitting in. I see her as arrogant and disrespectful.

After finishing her song, she and her companion walk up the incline to the raised boardwalk where they can be better viewed by the large crowd forming. It's not possible to tell whether her companion is a man or woman. Together, they launch into another song. Their performance is breathtaking, and in spite of my reluctance to grant them any recognition, I am drawn into watching. The music seems like a kind of bluegrass, and even though no one is playing any instrument, I can vividly hear guitars and banjos accompanying them.

On the next number, the asexual-looking one takes out a strange-looking instrument, something resembling a dulcimer, playing sparsely on it. The song is again enchanting and otherworldly, lifting me into an exalted state. The second performer takes off the hat she had been wearing, revealing that she is also a woman. They go on with the performance, introducing more instruments, completely winning the crowd and me, stirring us with the transcendent, effervescent beauty of their song.

Then, the second woman talks to the crowd. She tells us that her partner, the one who first attracted our attention by singing on the corner, is to be executed in two days by the judicial system for a crime she has committed. She has been allowed out of jail for this performance as a special last favor. We are further told the performance has been her way of saying good-bye and giving back.

As I look again at the first woman, I see her in this new perspective. I now understand her radiance, her abandon, and the power she has had over us. She is positively glowing with peace and love. There is no doubt she has accepted her impending death and has been empowered by it. The light surrounding her has affected us all, lifting us to the higher vibration. I have come across this kind of experience in films or books, where the hero bravely faces annihilation, but to see it here in front of me, for real, is completely moving. Her power is overwhelming. I stand watching, absolutely transfixed.

FLYING

Throngs of people are milling about the grounds at the annual state fair. It's midwest summer, sunny and hot. There are many booths with intricate displays and games. In an open field there's an air show with various types of planes taking off and landing. As the crowd watches nervously, a twin-engine jet convulses in for a landing out of control, ending up unharmed in tall grass. Upon closer inspection, however, it turns out to be only a realistic model.

In another part of the field, there's a ride that takes people up in the air. A helicopter is stationary overhead with a cable running down to an old powder-blue convertible car on the ground. People get in the car, and the helicopter pulls it off the ground. After releasing the cable, the car then flies off on its own, miraculously soaring above the fairgrounds, almost out of sight at times, with no apparent means of propulsion.

I consider going up for a ride. Although I'm not sure about flying in an old car, it seems everyone else is enjoying it, so I decide to go ahead. Another old convertible, a Ford from the fifties painted primer-gray, lands with a crunch and people jump out. I climb in with others, and we wait for the ride to begin. Soon, the car lifts off the ground to a height of about ten feet, swaying back and forth. I look up to see we are suspended from a large crane with a scissors-extension type of arm and a double claw scoop at the end skillfully painted to resemble a dragon's head. The cable holding us leads out of the dragon's mouth. We just keep dangling there, barely off the ground. I seem to be the only one who notices we are not really flying, just hanging. Everyone else is having a wonderful time.

The ride ends. I get out of the car, disgusted at being cheated, and decide not to pay the $3.50 for the ride. I just walk away. Secretly, I am glad to have found an excuse to avoid spending the money. But as I walk, I start to feel I am being followed. I turn to see a few attendants from the ride, who I now realize have noticed I did not pay. Their tactic at this point is to keep shadowing me.

Walking on, distressed, I stumble carelessly into some kind of game booth, becoming caught in a series of strings stretched across the booth at knee level. I sit down to excruciatingly disentangle myself as they watch, amused. I start walking again, now with more attendants behind me. I hear them discussing what to do with me. They want to catch me and lock me in a dark room upstairs for a month.

I run down a narrow aisle with people and booths packed on both sides, but they are right behind me. I snatch a crowbar I see leaning against a wall. I strike out with it, holding the bar in both hands at the bent end and swinging back over my head as I run. I hit one, then another of them. These two go unconscious, slowing down the others who have to climb past them. I run faster, into a shop that appears to be a jewelry store, diving over counters, dodging people, finally seeing an exit to the street where I fear there will be a guard who will snare me. I get to the exit and see no guard. I run out into the street, using the crowbar as a cane to help me go faster. As I pole along, I frantically look for a cab to make good my getaway.

LOFT

There are windows on three sides of Lester's loft so you can look out. There is also a door, so you can walk out onto the fire escape. Lester is pleased with the loft. He's sitting at his drawing table with the small flexible figures he uses for models. He moves them until he gets an interesting angle to draw. They are figures with curves, and he draws curves. He appears to be angry for not having achieved success yet.

I am sitting in another part of the loft, with eyes closed and headphones on, listening to music. I feel an arm around me, across my chest, holding me. I don't recognize what it is at first, but then I realize it is Lynn, Lester's girlfriend. It feels good to be held, but I'm embarrassed because Lester is there. I keep my eyes closed without moving or responding because I do not really want Lynn.

Lynn and I leave the loft and walk towards the river. Lynn hints she will leave Lester for me. I don't want to tell her I'm not attracted to her, so I just say, I don't know. As Lynn and I walk, I slap her on the ass in a friendly way. It feels better than I expected.

We walk out onto a dock over the water. As we get to the end, I fall off. I keep myself from falling quickly, going over slowly, pivoting like a tree falling in the forest. Before I hit the water, I remain suspended horizontally over the surface for a minute. The balancing sensation is delightful. Other people on the dock are amused. As I get back on the dock, I notice some people are nude (it is quite sunny). I'm glad they feel free enough to do that, although I don't participate.

RUNNING

The gym is a huge space, full of people engaged in various activities, all going on simultaneously. There's an area where groups of three men are furiously wrestling together in a strange style. An unusual type of basketball game is underway in another area. Not everyone is drawn to take part in activity, however, some are just standing on the sidelines, watching. Then, a long section of floor in the middle of the gym turns into a treadmill. People nearby start running in place. This appeals to many of those standing and watching, so they go over and join in. The treadmill gets crowded with all kinds of people, young and old, men and women. They are all running together.

After a time, the treadmill slows down. The crowd is uncomfortable with the new speed; it seems too slow for running, but too fast for walking. As they try to adjust to the speed, they discover a new kind of movement, neither running nor walking, but something in-between. The movement seems cartoon-like, with legs moving resembling horses trotting, steady and even. They find the movement is stretching their bodies in new ways, working out knots of which they'd been unaware. They find to their surprise that they like the new type of locomotion.

As the group continues to move, a section of wall opens before them. They leave the gym and enter a winding hallway. It looks like the inside of an old castle, with gray stone interior and dim lighting from torches fixed on the walls. After a short distance, the hallway opens into a wider area where a rock band is getting ready to play. The band is fussing around with their equipment, waiting for the right time to start. One of the runners shouts out "all right let's hear it," thinking they might need encouragement. Everyone is surprised that, contrary to the banality of the words, his voice seems to have acquired a tremendous tone of authority, presence, gentleness, and inspiration. The band reacts as if some cosmic being has spoken to them – they immediately get in place to begin. Everyone is amazed so much has been transmitted in one short phrase, amazed at the change in the voice from its usual speaking. They linger with the memory of the sound, hearing it over and over in their minds, repeating it like a mantra, enjoying its vibrancy, depth, and power.

The band begins playing. They play *Blue Suede Shoes*. The thinking of the crowd switches from needing to run to get somewhere else to enjoying being present now with the band. This shift of consciousness seems to also have been engendered by the speaking. However, the band appears to be, again, playing the song too slowly. The crowd is unable to let go into the frantic kind of dancing they are used to. Instead, they fall into doing calisthenic-like movements in time to the music, with restraint and steadiness, similar to the new running/walking. Soon, the movement seems natural.

HIGHER ORDER

A young man is invited to a small dinner party. There are two other people there, both older, a woman with grayish hair whom he finds appealing in a non-sexual way, and another man. The man is talking about various things, making interesting occult insights. The party is joined by others; lively discussion ensues between individuals of the group. People keep moving around the table so everyone is always next to someone new. The crowd is older, but the young man finds them quite engaging. They are talking about occult matters.

The group keeps getting larger. The young man gets the feeling the occasion is for his benefit; he is being introduced to a mystical group; he is becoming part of something, an insider. He is elated he will no longer be isolated.

During the course of the evening some people perform a short play, turning into other persons – younger and more stylish. They move around with utterly carefree and happy expressions. The young man meets other young people who assure him the group is really a higher order.

COINS

A man and woman sit at a sidewalk café at 3 a.m. in a large city. The streets are dark and deserted. She tells him she's going to give him the chance to win his money back. She's going to throw three coins; if they all come up with the same side, he wins. She throws, and he wins $150. She gets ready to throw again, but he interrupts, saying he thinks she is deliberately throwing them so he'll win. He shows her how to shake the coins in his cupped hands, and he throws them this time. He wins again.

DENTISTRY

I need a new way to make a living. I decide to become a dentist. Because I have had a lot of dental work done on me, I determine I won't need any formal training in dentistry. I just set up an office and start working on patients, letting my intuition guide me.

Things are going well, when the husband of a female patient calls to tell me he wants to talk with me. He comes over to the office. It turns out he's a dentist also, but his wife doesn't trust him enough to let him touch her teeth, and he's too nervous about working on her to be able to treat her anyway. He wants to know what it's like to work on her. As I discuss my impressions, he laps them up eagerly, vicariously, voyeuristically.

After that, however, the tone of the conversation takes an ominous turn. He discovers I don't know the correct names for any of the tools I use in my practice. He offers to pay me for his wife's last appointment, handing me a 100 dollar bill. I feel somewhat demeaned with taking cash, and as I look closely at the bill, I see it's a fake. Clearly, he is telling me I'm also a fake. He leaves the office in a huff.

Devastated, I go out for a walk. As I'm walking, it becomes harder and harder to move. I feel as if I'm encased in some thick fluid, as if my limbs are lead. It takes such an effort to make the slightest, slowest movement. I despondently drag myself along the sidewalk.

I pass a building I had not previously noticed. It appears newly built, in a neo-renaissance Italian style. As I look more closely, I see it's a public museum, so I go in. There is no art currently on display, but I find myself unexpectedly enraptured by the interior of the building. I see beautiful arches, walls painted pastel orange, ornate but modern-feeling white detail trim, large airy spaces, tremendous light coming in through octangular paned windows high up. I feel myself being restored by the power of architecture. I sit there until I am well again, and then go back to my office.

GEORGE

I am with George again, after not having seen him for a few years. The last time we spoke he looked unhappy and held-down. Now, he is radiant. His face has changed so his smile is magnificent and his expression beautiful, as if he has become a higher aspect of himself. I feel the immense love I have for him. I start opening inside with tremendous explosions of the heart. I feel bursts of emotion a quantum level above my normal perspective – crying, laughing, loving, releasing. The vibration takes me to a new level, lifting me out of the circumstances in which I have felt trapped; I have transcended. I see that death has finally resulted in a transformation for him, and that he appears to have gone beyond the pain and confusion he experienced in life.

I try to play some tapes of music he has composed and recorded, but the tapes are blank – no music comes up.

FLOWERS

Twelve year-old Jimmy has just given his mother a bouquet of flowers for Mother's day. She tells him it's not enough. She wants him to pay for a new cocktail dress she has in mind.

They are standing in the kitchen. He is aware of his attachment to her and becomes upset and angry because of her demand and his obligation. He starts throwing pieces of crockery on the floor, smashing them, although he would like to throw them at her. He has been working hard, cleaning the car, but she won't accept his work, she wants money. The rejection of his devotion is what gets him mad.

Then she becomes much younger and beautiful. She implies she is having an affair with some man other than his father, and this frees her spirit. She smiles in a way he has never seen – very happy. He asks her why he can't touch her breasts; after all, she is his mother.

SUBWAY

At the entrance to the subway, plainclothes police are spot-checking bags people are carrying. They ask to see Frank's bag in a charming way that surprises him. As they examine the contents, they find a gun. They tell him the gun is illegal and take him into custody.

At the station house, they ask him questions about his activities. He's frightened because even though he never planned to do anything with the gun, it looks bad. Finally, they tell him they are not really concerned about the gun – it is too old and rusty to be of any threat. However, they want him to be cleared by one more department before he leaves. He doesn't trust them and becomes frightened again.

ENCOUNTER

A small cruise ship is anchored for the day, off a deserted coast somewhere in New England. It's summer, but the day is cool. Passengers are mingling on deck, sheltered by a light wooden canopy. There are chairs and tables with food.

He goes up to her and initiates a conversation. She is wearing a bulky dark sweater with gray slacks. They continue talking for a while, getting along well. He feels his attraction for her quickly growing. They tacitly agree to stay together, walking around on the boat to see a different view or investigate a new activity. He finds he wants to get closer to her. At one point, he sits next to her, putting his arm around her. She responds by cautiously putting her arm around him. Becoming encouraged, he tries to get closer, but she resists. He realizes he is pushing too hard, too soon, trying to possess her, making her defensive. He sees the compulsion within him to control her and own her.

As he softens the grasping inside, she responds by becoming warmer. It feels utterly delightful to him that she is choosing to be near him without his having to psychically manipulate her. They are leaning against a varnished rail, arms around each other's backs, looking out over the water. It feels incredibly intimate to him. He revels in the beautiful feeling of simply being close to another person.

He tells her he's finding it difficult to distinguish between fantasy and reality. As he speaks, he realizes he is not being clear about what he means. He's trying to explain that he's experiencing a new sense of continuity between his inner and outer sense of being, that they no longer seem to be split as they used to, and that the fantasies somehow carry over into reality. He becomes apprehensive, thinking he has said something that might alienate her, but she replies she knows exactly what he means, she feels the same way. He feels even closer to her.

They spend the entire afternoon together. His feelings keep growing stronger. It seems to him time for them to move to the next stage. He gently takes her by the sleeve and pulls her in the direction of the cabins below. She smiles brightly, allowing herself to be led. They go down the narrow stairs to the passageway leading to her cabin. He tells her he'll meet her inside the cabin as he opens the door to the head in the hall. She continues down the passageway. As he watches her walking, she loosens her pants so they drop completely off her onto the floor, leaving her bare butt not quite covered by her sweater. She knows he is watching. She turns her head and gives him a quick, sultry smile as she glides into the cabin.

He is excited to a state of frenzy. He stumbles wildly into the head, needing to take a leak badly, but discovers it full of luggage. He is unable to get to the toilet because of suitcases piled up. He stands there, stymied. He becomes annoyed at the inconsiderateness of the people who used the head for a locker. He opens the door and angrily starts throwing suitcases out into the hall.

As he's doing this, he sees his woman back out in the hall, outside the head. She has put on shorts and a sweatshirt in place of the sweater. She is smiling vapidly, as if she has no conception of what he thought they were leading up to. She doesn't seem to have any feelings she needs to take care of. She doesn't give any hint she is aware of any strong feelings in him. He is devastated with disappointment. He has no idea what to do next.

FAST

Sing the song bluebird Never more a token of Relay the intent Backward homespun Is the phone going to ring Cough sneeze blow out smoke Part the drapes Outside is cold Snow in L.A. Washing wood and sawing clothes Feet on the ceiling – they move around a lot Deb moved the laundry into the dryer So what Let's go I don't know if it matters A damn busted on the cherry trees The intense wavering of the poppies left me feeling ill at ease The red roof was not waterproof and the rain came in Let soup equal bread Tangent plus sine never mind It's all academic Too fruity too loose the goose I'll leave when the crow flies towards the sun It's never more to begun The empty house of horrors stood waiting for a laugh Psyched out by the seagulls She lay in a green pool of blank Don't you see it can't be real They're only pretending to like you Follow me up that hilltop where I parked my car last night I think It's the dark dirty one with no horn Symphony sympathy it's all the same when you can't get the record going The light from your camera hurts my toes Watch out But don't stop telling me you care I need a fast food something soon I need to stand in line and order from a high school dropout I need to carry my food through the crowd to a messy table and sit next to a family I need to be part of Or maybe just move on down the highway to the mall

SUPERMARKET

When I go to the supermarket, I'm surprised to see a sign saying it has become clothing-optional. I decide to join in, and take off my clothes. I'm shopping for just one meal: a salad with tuna. As I'm looking for the tuna, I come across another canned fish product. I read the label on the can. It tells me that if I eat enough of this, I will become immune to shark attacks. It seems the fish I take in becomes enough a part of my body so a shark will think I'm another fish and not a human when I'm in the water. The substance in the can consists of tiny shrimp in a pureed base of other unidentified sea creatures. I become nauseated at the idea of eating this mixture and put it back on the shelf. I become conscious of my penis dangling as I walk through the store. Then I notice nobody else is actually naked. Embarrassed, I get dressed and finish shopping.

LAUNDRY

I'm in a laundromat in Florida doing my laundry. The machine gets stuck after the wash cycle. I call the manager over. He tells an employee to take the clothes out of the machine and put them into a dryer. I become indignant, trying to explain that the soap has not been cleaned out of the clothes and they need to go through a complete cycle again. He doesn't agree or understand. I grab him forcefully by the throat, dragging him to another machine. He tries to strike out, but I dodge his fists. I warn him he should be careful – he's messing with a martial arts expert. Other people in the store become rowdy. A glass is thrown, landing on the floor, shattering explosively but smoothly.

I go back to the place where my father is sitting. He quotes a poem to me, surprising me since it is so completely out of character for him. The poem is a limerick about living in South Florida.

75,000 people live in this town.
They share 10,000 lawns all around.
1000 swimming pools in which to dunk,
and 3000 washing machines to run amuck.

MAGIC

Art takes place in a part of the psyche different from normal awareness. The experience of art is similar to the playful state of the child, or to the quietly involved, inner absorption of the meditator, or to our nightly surreal dreamworld, or to the sudden fascination that arises when we meet with a new, exciting person or circumstance, or simply to the spontaneous flight of inspired imagination. Art is magical. To understand it, we must have an appreciation for the magical realm.

The magical realm does not have the rules, boundaries, or logic of the ordinary world. Its keynote is that it is highly *subjective*. Entering it, we deliberately shift from outer orientation to inner orientation. We awaken our intuition, our emotion, our passion, our imagination. We become sensitive to subtle psychic currents usually unnoticed. We find stories, images, and sounds of a fantastic nature. When we develop sensitivity to the magical realm, we are tempted to stay there for as long as we can. We feel closer to the core of life, we feel more alive, we feel creative and rich in comparison to ordinary materialistic consciousness. We simply feel.

The essence of the magical realm is feeling. Through feeling, we perceive meanings, connections, and causes. Through feeling, we sense our enhanced and expanded self. When we communicate here, we communicate mostly feelings. When we attempt to manifest feeling in the material world, we produce what is called art. *Art is the embodiment of feeling in perceptible form.*

We may create art for several reasons. We may simply appreciate the joy inherent in the creative, expressive act itself. We may use art as a means to know, accept, and heal ourselves as part of our evolutionary growth. We may intend to communicate, to share with or influence others. We may find as we linger in the magical realm that feelings burst into consciousness, demanding to be molded into a certain medium for no logical or apparent reason.

When we approach the art of another, we must do so with much the same orientation as the artist did in bringing the work into manifestation. Of primary importance is opening to the feeling held in the work. It is not enough to simply appraise art with an analytical eye — to evaluate if the work has been properly done, or to compare it to other works, or even to analyze what the message might be or to search for meaning. Art does not happen in the domain of appraisal or analysis. These are what have come to be called left-brain functions, meaning an orientation of the intellect. Art takes place in the right-brain, otherwise known as the magical. Tragically, most of us are not even aware of right-brain possibilities because all of our lives have been spent in the left-brain. We strive, plan, seek, reason — activities that are of course necessary, but which we have allowed to dominate and suppress the higher right-brain magical consciousness and keep it dormant.

The intellect is a tool of the ego and usually seeks to *gain*, if not materially, then in more subtle ways. The motive of gain keeps us trapped in the limited ego-self, which is primarily associated with the time-bound consciousness of the left-brain, and we are unable to truly engage art, as well as any other experience presented to us. Realization of the extent of our entanglement with and liberation from the seeking, gain-oriented left-brain enables us to enter *the moment*, which is primarily associated with the right-brain. *The moment* is that place where perception is not cluttered by the time-based thoughts of the mind but instead, rests unpreoccupied, able to open on the feeling level to any chosen stimulus, such as the work before us. *The moment* is where art happens and is the home of the magical feeling capacity.

Feeling is always an integral part of authentic art, but this does not necessarily mean the artist has intentionally tried to "express" a certain feeling in the piece. Rather, in powerful art, the artist has allowed *universal* feeling to enter the work. This happens even if the artist starts the work in order to explore a personal issue. The work takes over, and the artist becomes more of a "channel" than a source. The work may take on qualities the artist never foresaw; this is one of the more delightful aspects of creating art. The more direct the representation of universal feelings, or what are also called *archetypes*, the more powerful the piece becomes. The work comes alive, even assuming an independent existence. As an independent entity, the art piece can be interacted with by another person approaching in the magical realm.

The capacity to engage art develops as one becomes aware of and interested in the possibilities inherent in this type of consciousness. The act of creating art is, of course, a primary way to cultivate the magical, but one need not be a practicing artist to have developed the facility; there are other paths to the development of artistic awareness. What they all have in common is a deliberate altering of consciousness, usually starting with relaxing, winding down, and shifting to a mode of inner awareness centered in feeling. For example, you could invoke the state by remembering what it was like to play as a child. Children at play exist in a highly magical state. They interact with beings of their imagination as much or more real than those of the material world. They imbue ordinary objects with extraordinary identity and power, performing the basic artistic act. Children are primarily in the right-brain. At a certain point, the shift occurs to a predominately left-brain orientation with the onset of adulthood.

Or, to enter the magical realm, you might use body-oriented techniques. You could start with yoga-type breathing to change your brainwaves to more of an *alpha* rhythm, where feeling, healing and creativity occur together. Then, focus on the body to bring yourself into a grounded place, out of the thinking mind. As you enter body feeling, allow yourself to continue through to the higher psychic sensitivities of the feeling self. The key is to place yourself in a deeply relaxed state, and then allow feelings to come up spontaneously, stimulated by the art.

Spiritual and consciousness development paths in general including meditation and therapy will work to activate the right-brain and increase feeling sensitivity, especially if used with that purpose in mind, and so can prepare one for the experience of art. Basic meditation techniques such as repeating a mantra or keeping the attention on the breath will help to quiet the chattering mind and shift to the right-brain. But as you sit in meditation, don't think your experience has to be completely empty. When you sit quietly, either in meditation or in contemplation of an art piece, feelings that need to be released from the subconscious will jump into awareness. It's important to not become upset or impatient when such feelings come up, especially if they are uncomfortable; instead, realize that the feelings are attempting to clear themselves.

Practice simply being with, in a peaceful and accepting way, whatever feelings arise, whether harmonious or what we usually think of as negative or painful. Keep away from analysis of the feeling for now. Do not be afraid to open to the feeling, whatever it is. It is the opening to and experiencing of feelings, *witnessing them without resistance, blame, or acting them out,* that eventually releases and balances them. Learning to choicelessly open to your feelings as they are, with no editing, is the essence of developing the magical feeling capacity for experiencing and creating art and opening to the higher energy planes, as well as resolving and transcending those feelings and the associated karmic life circumstances and advancing on the inner path.

Often, we don't really allow our feeling selves to come forth and develop. Instead, we *suppress* those feelings and urges that we perceive as painful, violent, selfish, or otherwise unacceptable, pushing them out of conscious awareness into what is called the subconscious, even perhaps because they do not fit in with our unenlightened image of what it means to be a spiritually evolved person. Instead of integrating these elements into a complete, mature experience of ourselves, we hide them, creating our *shadow* self, and development of our feeling sides becomes stagnated.

Although I am not recommending it, it should be noted that alcohol and certain drugs may loosen the door to the creative. Occasional, judicious use of such stimulants may not be harmful, but their use often gets out of control. As a result, there exists an abundance of artists with histories of substance abuse and the backlash depression that comes from the stimulant's depleting the psychic energy reserves in order to produce the high. There is really no need for these dangerous substances.

Intelligently working on yourself will lift the blocks to feeling and creativity, and even yoga breathwork can do a great deal to safely facilitate the same kind of consciousness shift that the stimulants provide.

But what's most important is to remember – to keep consciously reminding yourself – to approach any art from the right brain, magical place. Observe yourself as you sit in front of the art. Are you evaluating it, thinking about it, comparing it to other work, are you seeking, perhaps unconsciously, to understand what it means? This is the orientation of the left-brain, and you will never get far with art if you do not transcend it and move to the right-brain. Come into the moment, and let the art wash over you. Have an *experience* of it. Jump into the river of life instead of sitting on the bank, never getting wet. Consciously put thinking aside, and allow feeling to come forward; replace reason with intuition, analysis with empathy, and meaning with magic.

As you enter the magical, you become susceptible to the drama of the work; you allow it to lead you; you surrender to its story; you deeply and empathically receive it. You resonate with the feelings in the art. Having learned to open and attune to the work of art will also mean you have acquired the ability to more directly open to yourself and others. However, for the work to be especially moving, two conditions must be met: The work must stimulate feelings that have up to now not been completely recognized, and to be even more powerful, the archetypes within ourselves must be touched.

PRESIDENT

Michael and Julie are prominent members of a well-known dance company in New York City. They are invited to put on a special performance at the White House for the President. Julie is excited because she wants to be seen as much as possible. She welcomes the opportunity to be recognized by such distinguished personage.

They do the show, and directly afterwards watch it on videotape. Inwardly, Michael winces as he sees himself, never being comfortable with how he looks. He also winces at seeing Julie because he is ambivalent about her individualistic dancing style. He is afraid to say anything to her about this, however.

Next, they attend a dinner reception. After dinner, there is ballroom dancing with an orchestra. The President comes over and asks Michael to dance with him. They face each other and tape their knees together with duct tape, the President's right knee to Michael's left knee, the President's left knee to Michael's right knee. They join arms, dancing intently with knees locked, taking turns leading, trying different steps, but never seeming to be able to fall into a smoothly coordinated pattern. They go on like this for about twenty minutes.

When they are done, the President tells Michael and Julie he has enjoyed their company immensely and wants them to come back for his inaugural celebration in one and a half years. They are surprised plans are made so far in advance.

Michael and Julie leave. He tells her he found the whole time trying, he felt no one was real, and he couldn't be real either. She tells him she is not sure if she wants to come back.

MEN'S ROOM

I'm in a public place and need to take a shit. I go to the men's room. It's fairly large, but has only one toilet with no privacy enclosure. I lock the door with the small hook on it because I don't want to be seen by strangers coming in as I'm sitting on the can but, before I can go, someone knocks loudly on the door. Thinking I could never relax enough to have a bowel movement with the commotion outside, I get off the toilet and unlatch the door. A man comes in to use only the sink to wash up. I decide to just urinate, to at least release some of the pressure.

I notice this particular men's room doesn't have the ordinary kind of urinals, but instead you just piss against one of the tile walls European style and it runs down along the baseboard into a floor drain. I try doing this, but instead of going into the drain, the urine splashes back on my pants and ankles, running all over the floor, getting my shoes wet. I finish peeing anyway. There are now other men in the room, looking at me strangely as I go over to the sink to wash. As I get to the sink, I notice the urinals placed around a corner where I hadn't looked. I wash my hands and leave the men's room.

THREE DREAMS

I'm the manager of a musical act. We pull into a town with our big trucks, going straight to the arena where we will be performing later in the evening. It's an open-air pavilion that will make for a pleasant show since it's summer and the weather is beautiful. This is to be a free concert, even though we will be paid by the sponsor. It's about eight in the morning, sunny and bright. People are already arriving, walking up fenced paths through the green grass to get good seats.

I go into town to run a few errands. As I'm walking down the corridor of a large office building, I pass an open door and hear the sound of ecstatic moaning. I look into the room to see that these noises are being made as an expression of pleasure/pain by someone receiving a massage. I am shocked to see that the practitioner giving the massage is a huge, hideous, powerful-looking reptilian creature with light green scaly skin, a fin down the back, and enormous webbed hands. The creature is holding the client with only one hand wrapped entirely around the client's back, apparently applying strong pressure with no movement at just the right points to be effective. The client is a man who appears to be strongly built himself. I can see his well-developed muscles since he is without a shirt. I stand there, mesmerized by the scene.

The massage ends and the client leaves. I consider that I could use a massage with all the stress I am under, but I am unsure about receiving it from this particular practitioner. Immediately, the creature changes form right before me, becoming a lithe, good-looking young man with short black hair, resembling a certain movie star. I find him appealing. I especially like the appearance of his hands. He explains to me that when he is working on someone, he assumes whatever form will be most effective for that person. This intrigues me even more, so I agree to a session.

I strip down to my white undershorts and lie on a foam mattress on the floor covered by a white fitted sheet and transparent plastic. As he is getting ready to work on me I become concerned about what the charge will be and I ask him. He replies sixty dollars for forty-five minutes. I agree, but then I remember I am dreaming, and it doesn't matter what he charges me – I don't have to pay him with real money. However, another part of me responds that a service is being performed for me here, and I will have to pay back in some way the value we have placed on it.

We begin. I tell him I like a hard massage, but he says my body is not ready for that. I allow him to work on me as he sees fit. As he proceeds, I realize he is not only manipulating muscles, but is also sending strong energy to places where it is needed. He senses an injury on my spine that has not been healing. His technique here is to tap lightly and quickly with his fingers in small circles around the hurt area. He senses my kidneys are weak. He grabs my body with both hands over the kidneys, holding me up off the mattress.

It feels supportive and nourishing to receive these treatments, especially the last one. I feel myself becoming healed on all levels. We change position on the mattress; at times he is sitting or lying next to me or even under me, holding me up with his hands. I realize the treatment is powerful and is affecting my self on earth.

Suddenly I wake from the dream. I want to remember all the details, so I grab a piece of paper on which to write. I put myself into a trance to recall what happened. In the trance, I find I need to move and write very slowly. I become aware of someone around me. My wife has gotten out of bed and is watching me write in my plodding, meticulous manner. I hear her moving around the room, but it doesn't bother me.

The phone rings. As the machine answers, we listen to a woman leave a hurried message – she needs some bodywork today, can I please see her? I remember I am a bodyworker. Still in trance, I ask my wife to pick up the call and make an appointment with her for later. I continue to write. When my wife returns from the call, she has become my mother. I am annoyed that she is intruding on my privacy.

Then, abruptly, I wake from this second dream. I lie in bed, completely still and frozen, unable to move or talk. I just remain aware of myself in my body.

Soon, I wake from this final dream. I am now fully back in my physical body.

MARRIED

Jimmy, age 34, is visiting his parents at their home for two days at Thanksgiving. On the first day, they tell him they've arranged for him to marry someone they've met, and he has no choice. He is enraged, thinking his parents still control him, but then he realizes he's mostly furious because of the humiliation he feels at not being able to find a woman on his own. He starts throwing dishes, smashing them against the floor and walls.

Jimmy's parents go out to trade in his car on a new one for him. As he's cleaning up the broken pieces, the woman he's to marry arrives; they meet for the first time. She asks him if he's lived long in this town. He replies that he grew up here, quietly admiring her inquisitive manner. He can't really see her body because of the long coat she's wearing, but it looks as if it might be nice even though he is uncomfortable that she is slightly taller. She has a pretty face with short, dirty blond hair that sticks out. She's wearing a black sheath dress under the tan trench coat.

Jimmy and his fiancé go out to a crowded restaurant. He notices she is the most attractive woman there, and finds himself wanting her. They are at their table, sitting on a banquette. He keeps trying to draw her close to him, but she keeps evading him. Finally he is able to get next to her. As he puts his arm around her, his hand accidentally slips under her dress. He becomes excited feeling her bare skin. She is still uninterested. He asks her if she's ever had sex. She becomes offended.

SMILE

And when it's time to jump on the railroad, move on down the track to the wrong side of town, emphasize the negative,

You left your toothbrush in the kitchen, willit get in the way?

Go back to the wrong train, pull the cord on the next frame, many a mile, desert isle

File, I'll, cry instead

Stage file, single file, secret file

Separate the best from the better. Margarine, plastic coated, leave the rest. Take all the promises left in the refrigerator, give back the extra portions of babo. Tie that bandanna, Dan, around your car. Let it happen, man. Dead pan, dirty pan, oh Pan.

Open it yourself.

I'm dreaming of a white corpuscle, just like the ones I used to know

Nile, pile, dial, bile,

file, tile, guile, vile,

while, rile, mile, trial,

isle, Lyle, style,   smile

ESCALATOR

I'm in a large department store on an escalator, going down. Right in front of me is a woman in a tight, satiny, yellow-orange floral print dress. I notice she has a great ass, so I step next to her and say hello. When she turns to look at me, I see her face for the first time. It looks hard. I'm not attracted to her face. She tells me she would never go out with me because my eyes are worn-out and hungry-looking. I thank her for telling me the truth. As I thank her, I put my thumb on her forehead in a kind of benediction. We reach the bottom of the escalator and she walks away.

NEWARK

A group of us are driving out of the city, across the George Washington bridge, going through Newark. We see panoramic vistas of urban getto – areas that look relatively unexplored by whites that make New York seem tame. There is a strong sense of restlessness and chaos on the streets. I think I would be afraid to get out of the car, but also realize that being here is illuminating.

We drive through to the country, to a store we are looking for. The store is crowded, with many rooms. It's an old barn structure, converted, with rough wooden interior and hazy yellow lightglow. The floor is sloping so it's hard to walk. At first I'm looking for a sink, but I forget that when I see unusual, well-made clothes and remarkable antiques. One room has beautifully made keyboards, some old, some from the French Renaissance, carved in cherry and lacquered. In another room, children are charmingly singing together to a strange song, more like a chant.

I find the counter for handguns. I'm shown a gun that looks like a camera – you keep it hung around your neck and when you press the button it shoots the unwise molester. It is also quiet. I look at other interesting handguns with black, compelling appearances.

I go downstairs to a room with a saleswoman, to inspect cloaks. When we are alone, I go up to her and touch her breasts. She makes some resistance. I feel her bra shaping them under her tight, thick sweater. I reach under the sweater and loosen the bra, continuing to caress her breasts, greatly enjoying the sensation. She keeps resisting slightly.

Back at the car, ready to go. Not everybody has gotten back, and we are thinking about whether to leave without them. Bill Boggs (whom I just saw on TV) is standing there, and asks me how old I am. I find it incredible he's 35 but looks older than me. He says I look older than him.

BRAKES

Jimmy is driving his parents in his van. They pull into his old high school parking lot. Usually it's crowded, but today they are arriving early and easily find a place to park, next to an old VW bug, painted dark red. As they pull into the space, he hits the brakes, but the car doesn't stop as quickly as it should. He jams the pedal frantically to the floor with all his strength, cursing out loud "These fucking brakes!" The car rolls too far, past the designated parking area, and the front wheels fall off the sharp edge so the bottom of the car crashes loudly onto the pavement. He asks his father if he has any suggestions about the brakes.

As they get out of the car, his mother tells him they have some money to get rid of, about $30,000, can he use it?

SHIP

A huge ocean liner passes near the coast of a summer seaside town. People on the beach are enchanted – ships this large don't usually come so close to land. As they watch, the ship starts to rise up into the air, presenting a perfect side view of itself with its neatly painted white upper decks, black hull, and immense red bottom previously hidden below the water line. It keeps rising slowly until it's high in the air where a small plane might be, hovering there while maintaining its steady forward movement, propellers spinning. People inland are also able to see the ship now that it has risen from the sea. Everyone stops, marveling at the incredible sight. People on the beach wave to those on the ship.

Then, slowly, the front end of the ship begins to tip down. Slowly, slowly, it keeps tipping over as if it is running off the edge of an invisible table. And as it tips forward it begins to fall.

The ship keeps falling and tipping until it is vertical in the air. It rotates further, like a slow-motion pinwheel, falling faster. Everyone is horrified for the people on the ship, that this is taking place in plain view and no one can do anything about it. The ship cartwheels down and lands upside-down in the ocean with tremendous impact. People inland are unable to see the crash because it's below their line of vision.

MOTORCYCLE

I bring in my motorcycle for repair. The shop tells me that instead of taking it apart, they can just put it into a large vat and run a certain fluid through and around it to restore all the parts to new condition – it's the latest breakthrough in technology. I agree to this. I watch through a glass panel on the side of the vat as the cycle is flushed and renovated. I see the energy of the fluid as it rushes around the machine, miraculously transforming it. When the cycle is removed, it looks wonderfully shiny and black, as if brand-new.

I settle the bill and get on the bike, heading out to the country. It's springtime, sunny, and the land is green and pristine. After driving a short distance, I get swept up in the physicality of the moment and decide to take off my clothes. As soon as I get naked, however, I become concerned about sitting with my bare asshole on the seat, thinking this is unsanitary and will get the now brand-new again seat dirty. I solve the problem by sitting on my tee shirt. I ride through the countryside, getting more and more into the sensuality of the machine, allowing myself to get an erection as I drive on in wild abandon. I see a group of people ahead. I'm apprehensive about how they will react to me, but they give me thumbs-up as I pass.

AND THE WALKING

The day lapses into evening. I pull onto a dirt lane lined by trees on both sides, running up a long incline through open fields. Ahead I notice a solitary black man walking with his back towards me. I gun the engine in order to pass him, but the bike hesitates and then stalls completely right next to him. It's dark under the trees as the black man turns and approaches me. I become frightened as I keep trying in vain to start the engine. As I look at the motorcycle, I see to my horror that much of the paint that had looked so shiny has fallen off, leaving only the orange primer and some bare metal. The black man lunges at me in an attempt to grab me. I respond by violently attacking him, twisting him into a lock with his arms over his head. He turns to mush, collapsing into the dirt. I warn him I know wrestling.

MIRROR

I'm standing in front of a large mirror in a diner. I have very long hair, parted on the side, and my face looks younger and different. Because of the incongruity with my usual appearance, I become aware that I am dreaming. I remember my goal is to have an orgasm. I see a woman with shaggy hair seated at a booth. I rush over and pull her off her seat. I tear off her jacket and shirt and press my face against her breasts, sucking them wildly. I smell her hair and body. I am at the verge of orgasm, trying to keep calm in order to not wake up, by separating myself as the viewer from the body becoming aroused. However, I wake up just before physical climax.

EUROPE

A crowded pub/restaurant/meeting place in Europe. There are interesting-looking women here. They dress exotically, seem open, soft, sexy without being vulgar. Some are sitting alone, as if they could be engaged in conversation.

The adjoining room is raucous – painted gray, dim and smoky with bare light bulbs hanging on black cords from the ceiling. A wild game is going on. Participants are in an area demarcated by a tall wire fence. The audience is sitting around the fence on bleachers, cheering passionately. It's some kind of slapping game – people inside the fence are slapping each other. It appears to make no sense. Another room beyond this one is full of antique carousels, pained and faded.

Frank leaves the pub. It's night, and as he walks down the street, he falls into an open manhole. He's horrified as he keeps falling into the blackness, thinking one of his worst fears has come true. But then, he stops falling. Somehow, his head pops up above ground with the rest of him stuck below the surface. He yells for help. Some people come over to rescue him. One of them says he could sleep at their apartment because hotels are expensive in London.

PAINTING

Bill used to be employed by an international computer company as a sales representative, but because of downsizing, he, along with many of his colleagues, one day found himself out of work. To maintain an income until he secured another professional position, Bill thought he might paint apartments. He posted signs in his neighborhood advertising himself.

When he went on his first job, he whimsically decided to wear his usual business dress, as a kind of ironic statement to himself. He painted for two days in a three-piece suit, white shirt and tie, shiny leather shoes, with personal grooming to match. He found he was able to work without getting even the slightest trace of paint on his clothes. His customers were pleased with the job, especially with how neat it was – there wasn't a misplaced drop of paint anywhere. They were particularly fascinated that he performed the job in a suit.

Because this job went so well, Bill decided to continue wearing business dress to his painting jobs as a promotional gimmick. Word of mouth spread about Bill's neatness. He was hired because of his reputation for good work, but also because people wanted to see if he could really paint their place without getting paint splashed on his suit. Soon, Bill had to hire some of his former co-workers to help him, after teaching them how to paint neatly in professional attire. He called his company *Painters In Suits*.

The painting concept took off beyond Bill's expectation. He tried to analyze exactly what was so appealing to people, reasoning there must be an unconscious, unfulfilled need for neatness into which he had accidentally tapped. The need for neatness must compensate for the general messiness, uncertainty, and chaos most people experience in the world today.

Sensing even more potential in the idea, Bill formed a performance art group. In the show, he and several of his colleagues appear on stage, dressed in their usual business outfits, and paint a complete stage set right before an audience. People are able to watch them actually execute the painting without getting a drop on their suits or the floor or the furniture or anywhere it shouldn't be. They always paint the set only one color, white, but vary the shade of the white so the new color can be discerned against the one from the previous performance.

Reviews of the show were astounding. Audiences raved about the Zen-like emptiness and precision of the experience, how as observers they spontaneously entered Satori, how they projected and saw and made peace with their inner demons against the blank screen of the visual spectacle, how they were able to finally trust that no paint would be splashed after years of psychotherapy had left them with still unresolved fear issues.

At this point, Bill has become an international figure. Items from the stage sets are shown at major New York auction houses and sold for hundreds of thousands of dollars amidst talk of their magical qualities. Bill has appeared on TV talk shows, and has been written about in pop magazines. He has led full workshops on how to attain high levels of neatness. He has met with spiritual and business leaders to discuss how to inculcate his philosophy in the general population. He is currently working on a book in which he explains the philosophy in detail.

UNCONSCIOUS

Art is a subjective discipline of bringing forth from the unconscious. In the unconscious of each of us lingers a vast reservoir of feelings unfelt, unexperienced, unlived. The unconscious, in broad terms, consists of both the lower, negative, *sub*conscious shadow material, which has usually accumulated because it has been previously suppressed; and the higher, exalted, *super*conscious aspects of ourselves into which we are growing on our spiritual, evolutionary path.

One of the idiosyncratic ways in which the mind works is that we will identify these unrecognized feelings, both lower and higher, in art objects as well as other people outside ourselves before we see them within. For example, if we are carrying excessive unconscious loneliness, we will be unusually sensitive to the loneliness portrayed in any work of art such as a film, novel, or song, as well as in another person. Or, if we have not been able to activate certain higher qualities in ourselves such as courage, sacrifice, or love, we will be enthralled by their depiction. In both cases, we are attracted to a reflection of qualities in ourselves to which we do not have direct access, but which we need in order to feel whole. This unconscious process is called *projection*. We become fascinated by the art because it provides the means for us to move toward wholeness as we recognize those unconscious parts of ourselves.

In addition, we may project and perceive feelings in the art that the artist never intended. We may see loneliness or love where there is none, and where other people do not. This does not mean we have misinterpreted the work. It is important to understand we have the capacity and the right to create our personal perception of the work. Indeed, the potential of the art to stimulate varying personal reactions of viewers is one of the qualities that gives depth to art, and one of the conceptual foundations of abstract art, with its high ambiguity.

We have gotten the impression that art is to be "interpreted." We think we must find what the artist is "expressing." Since art — especially modern art — is often obtuse, this search can easily become frustrating, particularly to one who is not well-versed in the language of art. This manner of approaching art may be relevant at times; there may be a message that should be heard, there may be a time to examine the psychology of the artist as represented by the work. However, this way of looking at art is unenlightened, limited, largely the result of our basically left-brain culture and a carry-over from when art was representational, and not even much fun. We look for intellectual content, for meaning and message when this is not really the point. The point is to engage art as a *direct experience*, on the feeling level. Liberate yourself from left-brain orientation; empower yourself by making the art your own. Drop the intellectual search, surrender to the art and let it work on you so you create your own significance.

Therefore, do not become preoccupied with trying to find what the artist is trying to say or what the meaning may be. Such an approach generally leaves us stuck in the left-brain. Instead, allow yourself to unconsciously project your own feelings into the work, recognize those feelings, and have an integrating and healing experience. The recognition, through projection, of whatever previously unconscious part of ourselves we see in the art is a tremendously emotional experience – it is why we are moved by the work. Our fascination can take several forms at this point:

If we have been working on ourselves, it is likely we have been focusing on shadow material, because that is where the work is to be done. We will be ready for and sensitive to the emergence of the negative through the art, and we will be accepting of the newly-recognized aspect of ourselves. We will feel more whole because we are connecting, through the art, to a forgotten part of ourselves. We will feel exhilarated, even if we are presented with what might normally appear to be a saddening emotional experience. We will be drawn back to the art, again and again, in order to re-experience the wholeness. We will gain a sense of calm and inner completion. We find in the art a *validation* of ourselves – it appears someone else has felt this way; we are not alone with this desperate feeling. We find courage to accept and *live through* our pain.

Moreover, and this is an important function of art, it gives us a sense of safety and ease to perceive the previously neglected part of ourselves outside of ourselves first, before we shift to the complete recognition that the aspect lives within and must be integrated. In this manner, we come gradually into wholeness. Otherwise, we might resist and never allow an abrupt recognition of the aspect within.

Other reactions to art are possible. If we are not particularly working on ourselves, we may be disturbed by much art, especially art that portrays the shadow side of the self as does the work in this book. And by the way, "working on yourself" does not imply that any abnormal dysfunction need be present, but rather means the intelligent activity of a person concerned with understanding and resolving the tremendous challenges, both inner and outer, with which we are all presented in life. We are disturbed by the art because we unconsciously recognize ourselves reflected in the work, but we have yet to come to terms with those aspects. Our limited but relatively stable sense of self is being shaken.

If this is your experience, I would urge you to consider the notions we have been discussing. Recognize that to go forward means to engage the dark side of your nature; that society is in turmoil exactly because we don't do this. And if you find areas of your life needing to be strengthened, the best way to proceed is to seek out the underlying subconscious feelings influencing you. This is the message of psychology and what Freud discovered. Unfortunately, however, the tendency to remain in denial is strong. Until we see the light, meaning that the problems we encounter originate within, we tend to dismiss any suggestion that working with the subconscious could have importance and that we, ourselves, could be in need of such work. We think it's the other who needs it.

Another, more exaggerated reaction to art and the stories presented here is one of violent aversion. If you have experienced this, it is safe to assume deep unconscious feelings are being stirred that need to be addressed. If you had no such feelings, you would not experience such a strong reaction – the work would pass by easily and you might even be open to being amused by the novelty of some of the images. A reaction of disapproval to any art is a reflection of self-rejection. This self-rejection occurs on the feeling level, and is the mechanism that keeps the feeling in the subconscious. The self-rejection carries over to anything that reminds us of those rejected parts of ourselves – people as well as art. We condemn the manifestation outside of ourselves, often with violent, righteous indignation: If I am not permitting myself to have this feeling or to accept this part of myself how dare you? Such is the basis for the intolerance we see all around us.

Allow yourself to go back to the experience of the unconscious. Let yourself be drawn into the dark, mysterious, feminine, magical realm. As you interact with the images presented here, allow your own feelings, fantasies, and hidden self to come forward. Understand that the story is only the stimulus to connect you to the depths within yourself. Be at peace with whatever you find.

ICE

The walls of Frank's apartment are gray with light green trim, the place looks old and beaten. There are several rooms. The front entrance consists of two doors that close together at a right angle. The police are outside, trying to force their way in to get him. He's holding the doors shut as they pull from the other side. There's a small hole in one of the doors through which they start pushing ice, in order to freeze him away, but the ice holds the doors stuck together instead. He realizes he can also latch the doors and doesn't need to hold them anymore. While they're still pulling, he's arranging his things to leave out the back door, which they don't know about. However, he has to change his pants, because he's wearing old work coveralls, and this takes a long time, getting his boots off and on, and so on. It is agonizing. He can't carry everything and has to leave behind two guitars. He gets away, all the time feeling very paranoid.

RECORDING

I go back to visit Martha's Vineyard, where I've lived for a period of my life. There's always been an artist colony on the island, ranging from New York escapee, getting-it-together types to the ultra-successful. What attracted me was the potential for taking part in a community, getting to know and bonding with a small group of people with compatible values as an antidote to my life as a loner.

As I look back upon my actual experience here, I recall that the ideal of community was never completely realized. I used to be bitter about this, but now I see it differently. Just that the ideal was able to be carried by the place, in my mind, is significant to me. It means that behind the scenes, somewhere on the astral planes, the ideal is real. As I'm visiting, the ideal seems to have come alive.

I'm wandering around, going nowhere in particular, when a musical phrase appears in my head. It's a bass line I find appealing. I keep running the line over and over in my mind, enjoying its energy, letting it propel me on my walk. I run into an old music buddy, Brad. I ask him if he happens to have a cassette recorder on him so I can record the phrase, because I know I'll probably forget it later. He says he doesn't.

We spend some time together, talking about music and the Vineyard. As evening approaches, we think about getting dinner. We go to a café where people congregate – it's a place where you order at the counter and carry your food to a table. It's Saturday night, and the place is buzzing, vibrant, warm. Music is playing. After a while, I notice that the music is coming from another part of the building, where there apparently is a recording studio. The room we are in contains recording equipment which seems to indicate that it corresponds to the control room of the studio complex. I see people at a music console. One of them is a middle-aged man with grayish hair, who appears to be the producer, running the session. I am told he's a local high school teacher. He looks like someone I could be friends with.

I learn that the studio and café were originally built as separate establishments but gradually coalesced into each other as they grew. It was found that recording sessions went better with people around rather than in isolation. People were free to drop into the café/control room at any time to listen, and sessions were scheduled for weekends by local musicians to coincide with the crowd, which was appreciative and supportive. At a certain point, some of the musicians came out of the other studio where they had been playing, and were overdubbing percussion parts in the café.

I'm sitting next to Brad and two other friends. We are leaning back on a sofa with our legs propped up on a coffee table, listening to the music. I'm on the outside of the sofa. The lighting is dim, the mood is dreamy and romantic. As I look at Brad, I'm astounded to see he has become someone else, a young, attractive woman with blond hair. His/her new face is remarkably familiar to me, although I can't quite place it. I realize I feel an immense attraction for this person. We turn towards each other. I put my arm around her shoulders and gently pull her towards me. Lightly, I caress her cheek and neck with my other hand as we gaze into each other. Simultaneously, I feel her hand touching me so softly though my pants. It is unimaginably exquisite.

WAITING

Because I have been unable to find happiness in pursuing or achieving anything, I stop pursuing and achieving and become catatonic, beyond communication. I become a crazy person.

I'm on the street, I fall down into a catatonic trance. Actually, what I'm doing is entering the highest degree of concentration possible, the highest I've ever experienced. It requires I absolutely forget everything else. I mentally take notes about what I see in the concentration. To describe the concentration is very hard, except to say that by resolving to inwardly do nothing, really nothing, I become entirely still. I choicelessly enter the catatonia.

I surrender to the street, to whatever will happen to me as I lie here with no defense. Fortunately, I'm in a place where I will not be robbed or attacked. It's crowded on the street, people are walking by. I'm lying on concrete steps in concentration, going deeper. I recognize I am still sane on the inside even though I must look crazy on the outside. But then I realize that, no, this must be what insanity is like – it's just that I am *aware* on the inside, which is not the same as being sane. Being unable to function is, of course, insane. I roll into different positions. I stumble down the street.

I'm adopted by a woman who looks after me. I have a car from before I became disabled, a new convertible, which she takes over, driving me. Later, two men adopt both of us in order to get the car. They drive with us in the back seat. I am still acting like an idiot, unable to talk or do anything, but I see with clarity. Since I am so unthreatening with my loss of will, they keep me around as a pet, finding comfort in my gentleness. We all live together in a house.

My catatonia represents my quest for happiness. In the catatonia, I wait to be saved by some unknown power. I wait without waiting.

FILM

Late night TV, a film about the Korean war. It is very well done. Soldiers are being pulled through dark water at night, hooked onto a floating chain.

One of their group is unable to attach to the chain even though it passes right by him and is left.

KICK

With Sylvie. We're pacing around in the apartment. She's mad that I asked her to stay on her side of the bed because I can't sleep with her hanging on me. Then I realize I've been dreaming the above. I'm in bed, lying on my front. She's standing over me on the bed and kicks me hard on my back with the bottom of her heel. It hurts, and keeps hurting. Angry, I respond by swatting wildly at her, but she's out of range. I wake from this second dream, the dream that contained the first dream. The room is completely calm. I wake her – she remembers nothing.

With Sylvie, in bed. I reach from behind her and stimulate her clit. Her cunt gets moist. I press my cock between her legs from behind, against her clit.

In bed with Sylvie. She's touched me on my shoulder, waking me and making me mad. She has done it affectionately, but I don't know that at the time. I grab her hand and violently fling her arm back. I go back to sleep, lapsing into a dream. She's lying on her back and I'm kneeling over her, straddling her, repeatedly slapping her as hard as I can. I lose control, I'm raging. I don't know why.

LEADER

It's Russell's last year in college. He's been elected leader of a men's acappella singing group of twelve members. They're about to leave for the Catskills from Ithaca, N.Y. for a four-day engagement during Christmas break. As he's packing, he happens to notice a professional quartet on TV performing one of the songs his group knows. They are splendid. They perform all four parts of the harmony vigorously and distinctly. He is intimidated by their excellence, knowing his group could never do as well. He hears them singing,

How could Red Riding Hood
Have been so very good
And still kept that wolf from her door, or, or, orrr?

The group is on the bus, cruising through the snowy landscape, when Russell is seized with panic. All the members of the group have been so busy lately they haven't had time to learn the extra material needed for this long engagement. Russell was planning to teach it to them on the bus; however, he now realizes that was completely unrealistic thinking – they will never be able to learn those songs in a few hours, on a bus ride. The engagement will be a disaster.

They arrive at the resort. Russell still has no idea what to do about his dilemma when he sees Todd, who was leader of the group in previous years before he graduated and Russell's good friend and roommate. Todd's exercising, running on the large snow-covered lawn. He looks quite fit, more than Russell remembers him. Russell falls in beside him, but since he doesn't feel like running, he just glides over the snow, the soles of his shoes brushing the surface, throwing up spray as he slides through small drifts. It's delightful, allowing him to forget his situation for a while.

Russell talks with Todd as they traverse the snow. Todd tells him he's come back to appear with the group and he'll take over, he'll pull the group through. He tells Russell he doesn't have enough musical skill to lead the group. Russell feels humiliated and inadequate, but relieved he's been saved and that his incompetence will not be noticed.

Later, as Russell is thinking about his feelings, he realizes in a moment of insight that Todd was his father in a past life. The experience of his sternness, the desire for and difficulty getting his approval, the reliance on his capacity, carry over from that relationship. Russell doesn't have the courage to tell him this.

HIGHER

The higher energy experience happened again last night. Out onto a new level of existence, feeling, and expression – a quantum jump above the usual. It's as if the vibration is turned up a few octaves, to a range where we don't usually pay attention. Everything is much quicker. It's euphoric, a kind of giddiness, a convulsive laughing jag far beyond the heaviness of ordinary life. It seemed closer than in other times, as if it might not be so hard to get back to.

I am appalled when I think about trying to relate to that woman last night. It was as if she was completely unreal and had no capacity to be authentic. But she seemed interested in talking. I can't even remember her name. I felt as if I was speaking of things deep and important to me, but she didn't recognize that. She responded with spiritual clichés.

BOAT

Boats have always been a fantasy of mine, so just after college I buy a big old power boat on which to live. I'm with my father and grandfather on the boat. We are moving it from New Jersey to New York City, where I intend to keep it. It's a clear dark starry night, January. We are traveling up the canals of the south Jersey coast, following the channel lights. I am inside the main cabin, steering. My grandfather, looking down into the engine hold behind me, sees something wrong with one of the engines. He suggests I look at it. I leave the wheel, but as I'm inspecting the engine, my father shouts we are going off course and heading for danger. I jump back to the wheel to see we have detoured into a side lagoon and are about to crash into the bulkhead at the end of it. I throw the engines into full reverse, and we stop just in time.

People in a house on the lagoon come out. They tell us we are in Holly Oaks, a town nowhere near where we want to be. They ask if they can come with us, saying they can show us the way back. I refuse, telling them we are under enough stress as it is, and I have a chart showing me exactly how to get back on course. My father, however, thinks it's a good idea to have them with us and tells them they can come.

Annoyed, I take my father aside. I tell him we are on my boat now for which I am responsible, and I am in charge. He doesn't seem to comprehend what I'm saying, but takes it as a personal rejection. I tell him emphatically again that what I want from him is his counsel, but I must make the decisions. He still doesn't appear to understand, and remains remote.

ABOVE

There's a thick crowd all around me. It's night, black with bright lights in the city. The crowd is moving in two directions on the wide sidewalk, making it hard to navigate through it. I'm trying to get to my mail in a 24 hour mailbox place. As I'm jostling through the crowd, I see a friend of mine, Paul. He's got shoulder length black hair and thick dark-framed horn-rim glasses on. He's standing, holding a clipboard with arms crossed over his chest, talking to someone in the crowd, a man he apparently just stopped on the sidewalk. The man is dressed in all black, a pull-over and pants. I overhear Paul ask him a question, "How many Jackson Pollack paintings have you seen in the last three decades – originals, not reproductions?" The man replies unhesitatingly, and Paul writes on his clipboard. I can't make out his answer, but I am somewhat intimidated, because I don't think I've seen any Pollack originals in the last three decades. Their conversation finished, the man departs.

I go over to Paul and we chat for a bit. He mentions there's the new Black-On-Black show opening Monday at the Modern. I make a mental note to attend. Then, he playfully launches into his artist-on-the-street role, telling me he's conducting an art project survey, asking if I would care to take part. I reply yes, impressed with his demeanor. Usually, he's fighting with his demons and is overwhelmed and unable to focus his strong talent. Now, he seems totally in possession of his higher side, and is exuding a confidence, vitality, and sense of purpose that has been attracting strangers and me into participating in his project. He has not told me exactly what the project is, but I am intrigued enough to believe it will be something meaningful, perhaps will be published, and I might like to be part of it.

He's rented a small room just off the street. We walk up to a second-story attic, with unpainted wooden boards on the bare floor and low peaked ceiling. There are a few light bulbs hanging from the ceiling, and school desks with attached chairs with people at them, writing intently. One woman is making a pen and ink drawing, apparently her response to the project. He tells me I have twenty minutes to reply, on paper, to the question. He asks me

"What if fear came from above?"

He gives me a notebook in which to write, in which other people have written, and leaves. Expecting to be asked the Pollack question, I am taken aback. The question is obscure to me – I am not sure what it is supposed to mean. What if fear came from above? – above what? I decide to scan what other people have answered, and to see if they were asked the same. I find that other people have written copiously, to the identical question. But then I realize it is lame to read others' responses in order to formulate my own. I should be clever enough to come up an original idea. I wonder if giving me the notebook with other people's responses was a test, or perhaps the whole project, to give me an insight into myself.

I try to move forward and to interpret the question. Maybe this is the nature of the project – to see how many different ways people will answer. What if fear came from above, and not below as it usually does, which is implied by the question. What does it mean if fear comes from below? It could mean that fear is part of our lower, disdainful selves – the part we want to be rid of, the part we fight with to make better. What if fear really belonged to the "above" side of ourselves, the higher side that contains all the goodness we hope to enjoy? It would necessitate a new way of looking at ourselves and the world. What if the negative came even as we sought the positive? What would be the purpose of continuing? The question starts to annoy me. The "above" side of ourselves, contains, by definition, qualities that are desirable, not qualities that make us unhappy.

I realize twenty minutes have passed. I anxiously await my friend's return, to collect my work. I have not begun to write. I am still struggling with the question.

ROAD

A group of men college students are lounging around a large dining table in their fraternity house. There's dark, ornate raised mahogany paneling on the walls and ceiling. They are all wearing dark suits and ties with white shirts. One student, Bob, is sitting quietly by himself when one of his brothers comes over and introduces him to a woman guest. Bob doesn't really want to be bothered, so he mumbles something, but is immediately embarrassed because he spoke incoherently. The woman, however, asks him to go for a ride with her, and for him to drive. After hearing her speak, he becomes interested in her, so he agrees. They go to her car, an old white two-seater MG with the top down. He drives it by sitting on top of the door, astride, pushing with one foot on the road while the other foot works the brake inside. It's dark night with stars. They are going down a deserted blacktop road with nothing but tall evergreens on the sides. After a half hour of driving, they arrive at the destination. They are about to turn off onto a long dirt road leading to a house when a man waiting there who seems to have authority tells Bob it would be better if he did not come in. Bob parks the car at the top of the dirt road. He's unable to see down the winding road because of the trees, and doesn't know what's happening there. The woman walks in without him.

RESTAURANT

I'm in a posh, crowded restaurant with a friend. We notice two beautiful women sitting at a small table, opposite each other – white tablecloth, bent chrome and wood/wicker chairs. White atmosphere. Flowers and modern paintings. They finish and leave the restaurant.

We go over to their table, sit down, and we discover their unpaid check. I do nothing, but my friend takes it to the cashier and pays it. The women, however, come back for the check and are thrilled with discovering my friend's having paid it without knowing them or expecting anything in return. They become quite warm for that reason and make a big fuss over him.

Then, I'm standing close to one of the women, and I can feel her body. The back of my hand is pressed into her thigh near her cunt, and I feel the exquisite lushness of her dress, the silkiness of her undergarments, and the softness of her leg. She doesn't seem to mind. I reach around and grab her ass with both hands – it feels luscious. My friend and I become completely involved with our women and unaware of each other. I don't know who this woman is. She remains passive.

GRAVITY

Three friends have formed a performance group. The unique feature of the group is that they have devised a way to avoid gravity. They are able to leap into the air and remain suspended for as long as they desire, which they accomplish by means of mind control. This ability has enabled them to come up with a new type of expressive movement, a synthesis of dance, gymnastics, tai-chi, and sculpture. Instead of being constantly in motion, which is usual in most body-oriented performance, they strike and hold a dynamic, expressive pose while floating about six feet off the ground.

For example, metaphorically portraying the soul's flight to freedom, one of them may vault into the air, holding a typical modern dance leap. The pose might change over time as the performer rotates slowly in space, illustrating various stages of the journey. Simultaneously, the performer is inwardly experiencing the escape from earthly containment the pose represents, usually with strong emotions. Their intent is for the audience to be able to experience with them the event portrayed by watching the movement as well as resonating with their feelings.

Each of performers is free to choose the event/emotion they portray, interacting with each other, the audience, and other intangibles of the performance environment, presenting a rehearsed but also spontaneous improvisational composition. Usually, each of the elements as well as the overall performance represents a dualistic, archetypal aspect of the human experience, such as love and loss, birth and death, fulfillment and tragedy.

They have made plans for a performance on the street, in a residential neighborhood during mid-day, when there are only a few people around. They are dressed in baggy, one-piece gray coveralls with paper-maché masks that cover their entire heads. The faces of the masks are white, expressionless, with holes for eyes, nose, and mouth. The backs of the masks have synthetic hair, coarse and red, like a clown's. They have found that using the masks helps to establish a mood of fantasy, and makes them feel more secure, since nobody can see who they are.

They begin the show, springing into the air, twisting into abnormal shapes, holding poses, bouncing off the pavement with one-handed cartwheels, delighting in the exquisite sensation of being able to express dramatic statements so completely though the body. They interact with the small crowd forming. One of the members, floating about five feet off the ground, feints striking out with twin karate kicks around the head of a spectator, who is amused. Another spectator, sitting at a bus stop, gives them a big smile. They feel encouraged by this approval, more than they expected, and realize how much they crave recognition.

They end the show, satisfied, and people disperse quickly since it's been raining for a while. The three of them leave in separate directions to go to their homes. One of the members, Russell, remembers he has to get in touch with his girlfriend Paula about getting together over the weekend. She lives upstate. He sees a phone outside a bar on a nearby corner and goes there to call her, but when he gets to the phone, he realizes he's forgotten her number. Not only that, but he seems to have forgotten how to use the phone, as well as how to conceptualize any phone number in his mind. Visualizing, sequencing digits as part of a longer, complex code is a mental task he can no longer carry out. He stands there struggling, trying to remember what the area code looks like, how many digits are contained in it, how many digits are in the phone number, how to use the phone, but his mind is confused. He feels himself slipping into a panic.

Russell remembers that Paula talks to his parents occasionally, and they would have her number. If he could call them, maybe they could help him. Then he realizes he has forgotten their number also. He has a notebook with him of personal information he gets out, hoping to find something there. He searches frantically through the pages, but only becomes more distressed, not recognizing anything. He keeps pushing with his mind, but to no avail. Finally, frightened that he losing his sanity, he breaks down in an outpouring of tears.

Despondent, he sinks to the ground, his head between his knees, crouching against the building in the rain. From within, an understanding presents itself: He has lost his rational mind capabilities as a result of having cultivated his artistic, feeling side to such a heightened degree. Exactly why this has to be, he doesn't know. However, he decides with abrupt determination that it's worth it. He will surrender to this fate if necessary to continue as an artist.

With resolve, he picks himself off the ground and goes into the bar in order to get out of the rain. The place is crowded and noisy. He sits at an empty table, just wanting to be left alone. Some of the audience from the performance are in the bar, and they see him without his mask, noticing he's been crying. He can tell they are wondering what's happening with him.

Then, to his amazement, he sees his mother on the other side of the room. She walks over and sits down across the table from him. He asks her if she has spoken to Paula. She ignores his question, telling him he is behaving very stupidly. She says that Mr. Simms, a teacher from the high school, called to say if he doesn't shape up he'll soon be in real trouble. She seems to think he is still in high school. He can't understand this. But what's most apparent is that she has no conception of where he is – that he had to sacrifice his rational abilities to avail himself of the higher artistic experience. She just keeps complaining at him, which makes him feel worse. He says he will try harder and walks out of the bar.

Russell resolves that since he can't use the phone, he will just drive to Paula's, hoping he will remember how. He remembers he has a car, which he has left in a parking lot. As he walks out of the bar, he space-shifts to a busy street in New York City. He jumps into a cab, to let the cab take him to his car. The cab is driven by a young, attractive woman. There's no meter in the cab, but she assures him they don't need one. They head west, over to Ninth Avenue, where he thinks his car is parked. On the way, they get caught in an immense traffic jam. After sitting locked in traffic for an hour, they decide to leave the cab and rest in a nearby hotel, planning to come back to the cab later.

As they talk in the hotel room, Russell finds he enjoys her company tremendously. She has such a high vibration that simply being with her is a complete delight. He definitely feels he is with an advanced being. He didn't think they had any intention to become intimate in the room, since he had told her he had a girlfriend, but at one point, she stops talking while looking directly at him with a beautiful, radiant smile. She keeps slowly moving closer to him, continuing to smile. Finally, she is so close she is only inches from his face. She kisses him. It's one of the most beautiful kisses he's ever experienced, completely unexpected and completely conscious. It lasts for about two minutes. He allows himself to kiss her even though he knows Paula is his true mate. After the kiss, they fall asleep.

In a few hours, they wake restored and go back to the cab. She drives him to his car. He finds he is able to manage operating it. He drives out of the city, heading north.

RIFLEMAN

Right now, I'd rather rent than sell, but thanks for asking. Situations, like grease, change with heat.

Getting a date is like fishing. If you jump into the pond, you scare the fish away. You have to let them swim up to the bait (you).

This is fun, now that I've gotten past my fear of wasting paper. I saw my reflection in the glass and didn't know it was me. I thought someone else was here. Scary.

Oh, I don't know, I guess I'll go back to sleep. Down to the bottom of the jar. Reckless thoughts are sometimes not easy to wipe out.

Super sam silly slit.

HYPNOSIS

Three friends are sitting at a table in a bar, drinking beers and fooling around. Sam shows Brad an advertisement in a magazine for a home hypnosis course that will enable the learner to persuade others to do whatever he wants. Sam is trying to persuade Brad to buy the course for him. He is leading him through a series of steps he has invented, calculated to bring him to the desired state of mind. Brad plays along as if hypnotized, saying things like yes master, but just before they get to the point where he is to sign the order form and give Sam ten dollars for the course, he stands up and tells him, still pretending to be hypnotized, to get some other asshole to do this for him. They all laugh.

SHADOW

The *shadow* is a term that refers to negative emotional and psychic energies that have accumulated and are held outside awareness in the area of the psyche called the *subconscious*. As humans, we have the capacity to store away these negative energies instead of releasing them. *The energies are released when they are fully accepted and experienced as feelings.* But we resist experiencing the feelings, usually because they are too painful or threatening, or because we just don't know any better. Instead of allowing the feeling to come into awareness, we reject the feeling; we push it away, we escape into all kinds of diversion, we never face the feeling fully. Because of this, the energy of the feeling is not exhausted; its cycle is not complete. The unfelt feeling energy does not go away but stays with us, trapped in latent form, becoming part of the shadow.

It is our instinct to turn from painful feelings; to not feel them; to *suppress* them – it seems part of our unconscious psychic defense system. But as we grow, we learn that what may seem instinctual and protective on a more limited level of consciousness evolution does not serve us on higher levels. Gradually, we overcome the temptation to reject our painful feeling selves and instead, open to those forgotten aspects of ourselves, reclaiming them, experiencing them in controlled and reasonable ways, releasing the trapped and built-up negative energies.

As we enter this process, we find that we go through stages of release, becoming aware of additional feelings behind the ones originally prominent. For example, behind our anger there may be fear or rejection. As we link feelings, we also gain spontaneous insight into other related dynamics of the self. We discover *patterns* of behavior – how we have been unconsciously motivated by the feelings in an attempt at compensation, and how this ultimately has worked against us. We may recall past experiences that have contributed to the formation of the suppressed feeling complexes, and so on. Our understanding comes by itself, without needing to search. We begin to clear on deep, psychological levels. We feel freer, more alive, more spontaneous and joyful.

Art can be used in this all-important work of self-healing. You start the process by noticing your reactions as you open to a work of art. If you find a particular piece that attracts you, it means the piece is stirring up a corresponding feeling in your unconscious. Allow the feeling to come. Welcome it. Do not be afraid – there is an automatic safeguard within that lets us see only what is right for us at any time. If you don't have an established practice of opening to your feelings, you may need to go slowly. Just be with whatever feeling comes up, whether it's one portrayed directly in the art or one that comes from within, triggered by the art. As you welcome the feeling, no matter how painful, understand it is coming from your subconscious shadow. It needs and wants to be recognized by your conscious self. If you can just be with the feeling, sitting with it calmly, even lovingly, detaching yourself from it while experiencing it, becoming the *witness*, the feeling will begin to clear.

Let the art take you deeper into the feeling. Keep the art as your focus – your reference to the magical inner realm, your grounding point between the feeling and the material plane. Continue being with the feeling until it shifts – until you experience it changing its nature and intensity. With strong feelings, you may need several sittings for them to clear. For important life clearing missions, it may take years or even a lifetime, but do not allow this to discourage you. You will find that the sense of moving in the right direction, clearing little by little, is enough to give you an optimistic and productive experience of life.

For example, to process the feeling of anger as portrayed in any of several stories presented here means that first, you are fascinated by the image because it portrays something about yourself that you may have been unconsciously rejecting. You may have judged yourself as bad for having this feeling, or you may have simply tried to push the feeling away in an attempt to smooth it over or to feel better. You are encouraged that you are not alone in having the feeling; someone else is familiar with it and has even written about it. You feel more of an acceptance of yourself and more of a closeness to others, because you see that we all have these feelings. You find yourself in the image and feel more complete. You may experience a flash of recognition of the full extent of the feeling, and how deeply and compulsively it has been driving you and affecting your relationships. Most importantly, you allow yourself to enter a right-brain feeling experience. Simply be with the feeling, witnessing it. At the same time, feel the anger deeply, *without blame or resistance,* allowing the feeling to dissipate as a result of its being experienced, and to lead you to deeper realizations concerning it.

One of the keys to successfully process any feeling is to have developed the capacity for *witnessing*. Instead of being enmeshed in the feeling, identified with it, we are able to step back and view it dispassionately, as part of ourselves, but not ourselves – we are something different. Developing the capacity for witnessing is a basic part of any authentic program for enlightenment.

There is no need to act out the feeling in any way. "Acting out" means yielding to the unenlightened impulse to express the feeling through action or interaction. For example, to be cruel because we are angry or hurt, or to indulge in addictive behavior or substances when we are lonely, or to mindlessly chase after money when we feel insecure. Our need to confront others in order to resolve feelings also changes dramatically when we have cleared feelings inwardly.

To take another example, at some point in the past we may have experienced a deep fear. If the fear was fully accepted and experienced, it would have cleared, but often we don't have the knowledge and presence of mind to correctly handle the feeling. In protecting ourselves, we unintentionally suppressed it, and it has remained with us in the subconscious shadow. "Subconscious" implies we are not normally aware of the full extent of the feeling, but it still influences us tremendously and from time to time will erupt and cause havoc. We carry the fear that was suppressed sometime in the past. We project the fear onto circumstances that do not really warrant it. We may have severe fear concerning money, for example, never being secure with what we have and always wanting more. At the same time, we paradoxically often sabotage ourselves from the attainment of what we are seeking, because the external condition cannot be improved until the inner feelings are resolved; it's the feelings that create the condition, not the other way around.

We are not aware that our fears are really unjustified; that they are actually coming from inside us. We think we would be happy if we could only get what we think we need. The first stage of enlightenment is to understand that it's not a question of attaining something outside ourselves. The fear is coming from the inside, and if we could resolve the inner fear, our experience of money and security would be entirely different. We would no longer be driven to acquire. We would be more at peace with what we had, and actually in a better position to attract prosperity because of our more evolved attitude towards it of non-attachment, and the absence of strong negative feelings that keep drawing it to us.

The same applies to all areas of life: relationships, achievements, and so on. If we are compulsively driven by inner unresolved feelings, we will never find satisfaction in attainment. We must first resolve the feelings within – those feelings held in the shadow. We all carry considerable quantities of personal issues that we need to address; this is a large part of our purpose on the earth plane.

Suppose we have been dealing with loneliness issues. Loneliness has been nagging at us and motivating us into futile compensating behavior. We may be aware of some aspects of the loneliness and how it motivates us, but usually we are not aware of the full depth. Since this kind of motivation is never successful, we are frustrated. When we have the experience of seeing loneliness in art, we may experience a flash of recognition of the full extent of the feeling. We see how deeply it is compulsively driving us. If we can allow ourselves to go one step further and simply allow the loneliness to be, if we can open to it without judgment, without blaming another for not being there for us, or without any other kind of shutting down or resistance to the feeling experience, the suppressed feeling will eventually clear. We say that the feeling has been *integrated*, because we dropped our resistance; and *cleared*, because the energy of the feeling will be released through experiencing it. Note this does not mean we will never be lonely again, because loneliness is a part of life; it just means that the suppressed, accumulated feelings have been released, and any "new" loneliness we encounter will be easily managed.

All suppressed feelings can be cleared by inner processing, and in my experience, this is the most powerful approach. It is amazing and paradoxical that simply by deeply experiencing the feelings, we dispel their power over us – they no longer drive us without our permission. We take control of our lives, and situations and relationships that seemed impossible to resolve through effort will miraculously and spontaneously change for the better.

This work becomes a very basic part of our evolutionary path. If not attended to, the suppressed negative affects us continually, greatly undermining our emotional state and even our physical health. It distorts our experience of life on all levels by highly coloring our perceptions and making us act and react irrationally and destructively, in more ways than we realize. In our work on ourselves, we therefore tend to emphasize releasing the negative. When this is accomplished, the higher levels of consciousness come forth spontaneously, without effort.

An important corollary of shadow work concerns taking responsibility for our feelings. Taking responsibility – *owning* – is one of the basic conditions of psychological healing work. When we see clearly that the feelings we experience are coming forward into awareness from their trapped place in the subconscious shadow, stimulated either by art or life itself, it becomes apparent that the blame we so easily apply to others when we feel mistreated by them is misplaced. Although others may be said to trigger our feelings, they are not the prime cause. We are the cause – we carry the feelings within, suppressed from some previous time, waiting for the right moment to be activated by circumstances and people we attract for that purpose. This is especially true with regard to any strong and recurrent feelings.

The implications of the shadow lead to deeper waters. It can be observed in psychological work that there tends to be a sharing of identical shadow qualities among people in general; even though we all have our *personal* issues to be worked through, there exists a *collective* sense of shadow material that must be resolved as part of our evolutionary path. This shared body of shadow material is part of what has been called the *collective unconscious*. It is important to understand that the collective unconscious contains higher transcendental elements as well as lower shadow elements; in opening to the unconscious, we therefore approach the superconscious cosmic as well as the subconscious shadow. We often don't see, however, that it is the very same blocks we maintain to the awareness of the lower shadow that keep us from the realization of our higher potential, as well as the accessing of our creativity in general.

As we explore the personal shadow, we come more and more into contact with the collective shadow. We recognize its universality; we see it's not only ourselves who has this hidden issue to be worked through, but we all do. We see clearly that we all are driven by fear, we all have repressed sexual issues, we all have immense anger that needs to be released, we all suffer from lack of recognition, poor self-esteem, and loneliness. In a way, it appears the personal issue that started us looking in a certain direction within is really insignificant when compared to the collective we discover. We may even be grateful we have experienced some particular difficult event, either in the distant or recent past, that caused us to begin the inner journey; indeed, that is the function of those events.

The realization of the collective shadow is an immense, breathtaking revelation. In a sense, it relieves us from the shame and guilt we may have felt in regard to our personal pain. We understand there is no reason for the shame and guilt – in an important way, the shadow I find within is not of my own making, but is something I have inherited with my humanity. What comes to mind is a new understanding of the ancient religious concept of "original sin." We have come into this world with a burden common to all, hidden in the subconscious and reflected through our personal issues and circumstances. The personal is only the particular way in which the collective manifests. Often, traditional psychological thinking assumes the shadow is composed only of personal, previously suppressed material; for example, feelings carried forward from childhood. Working within this paradigm can yield beneficial results in inner growth, but extending our vision to include the collective shadow can deepen our work, our compassion, and our connection to each other.

This does not mean we can fail to take responsibility for these painful experiences, however. The taking of responsibility is a crucial step in integration and clearing. When we include the collective in our *owning*, we broaden our sense of the isolated "I" to include all others. We empower ourselves by this step. Our concern shifts naturally to the well-being of the collective. We have grown.

CONSTRUCTION

Frank works for a construction company. He's assigned to a new job where he's supervising about ten people. They are renovating an old house. At lunch time, one of his workers, a woman, invites him to go out with her. She suggests they go to her place, which is nearby, and that she drive him on her motorcycle. Intrigued, he agrees.

Her bike is old, and looks like no motorcycle Frank has seen. It is large and clunky, painted dark flat gray, with a two-wheeled trailer attached behind for luggage. As they start to get on the bike, he wonders if her invitation has any sexual connotations; it will be intimate sitting on the saddle with her. She's wearing a short black leather jacket and long dark green plaid pleated skirt that she pulls up around her as she jumps on the seat and waits for him to get on behind. He does so, but is unable to figure out where to put his feet. He tries various places, and finally she directs him to what she thinks will be the best arrangement. They drive off.

They soon arrive at her neighborhood. It is crowded and run-down. There's an old elevated train track that runs over the busy main street. The track is in the process of being dismantled, so that part of the street is open to sunshine, but part remains shaded and dark under the ominous structure.

Her house is just around the corner. It is large, old, dirty, dilapidated, with other houses jammed right next to it. They go inside.

There are people inside with whom it appears she shares the place. They are mostly old with gray hair. They wander apparently aimlessly from room to room, drinking alcohol straight from bottles, passing the bottles around. Dogs are everywhere, some rolling on their backs playfully, but they add to the sense of chaos and distress that permeates the house. There's the faint smell of urine. Frank finds everything extremely seedy and repulsive. He wonders exactly who this woman is, and why she associates with these people. She doesn't seem to be one of them from outward appearance. She is younger, and works for a living, which it seems no one here does. He questions if she is drawn to this lifestyle for some inner purpose. Is this what she will become? Is there something she has to work out? But he doesn't see what it could be.

Continuing to feel completely uncomfortable, Frank walks with her through the house. They go from the hall into the kitchen, and from there they look through opened French doors into the living room. Here, in the middle of the floor, is a large bare mattress. On it are a man and woman, both naked. They are not in contact with each other, but seem to be in some sort of trance, either passed out or deep in thought or some other process. They are lounging in haphazard positions on the mattress – arms, legs, and torsos askew as if they had been dropped from above to fall as they might. The other people in the room seem to find nothing unusual about them, and continue to amble aimlessly around. A quiet somber mood fills the room.

Then, another person, a man, clothed, lies on the center of the mattress on his front. The other two rearrange themselves on either side of him, a few feet away, parallel but lower than him, so that if he were to put his arms out at right angles to his body, his hands would be on top of their heads. They all lie still. It's some kind of ritual, or exercise, Frank doesn't know what. But as he keeps watching, he gets the impression the man is performing some psychic act that is affecting the other two – that he is some kind of healer, therapist, shaman, or artist – but none of these labels seem exactly right.

Frank begins to sense something important going on; that these people understand why they are here, doing what they are doing. This further distresses him, because he's been noticing a sense of realness, honesty, and truth present that attracts him in spite of the sordidness of everything or, he thinks, is it because of the sordidness? He feels overwhelmed, intimidated, values shattered, out of his depth, suddenly aware there are parts of himself undeveloped and immature that he must seek out.

He realizes it is time to return to the job. He looks around for the woman who brought him here, but does not see her. He goes outside to discover her motorcycle gone. This upsets him more; he does not know how he will get back. Then he realizes he can take a cab.

ROYALTY

When Lydia was a child, she was treated like royalty.

Once, she went to take a nap in the afternoon. The bed was enclosed by a curtain around the sides and a canopy overhead. She lay on the bed and felt something big and hard under the pillow. Reaching under, she found a severed head, a man with a short red beard. Her hands were bloody. There was an uproar in the household about the head. No one knew how it got there.

CAFÉ

Loneliness. It's the feeling of not being connected to someone or something. The connection takes place on a level that could be called psychic, or inner, or emotional. The loneliness is often not within awareness, but still keeps compulsively motivating us to relieve it.

I'm in a coffee café in the new town where I've just moved. I know no one. There are others sitting around. A few men younger than me look interesting. Interesting to me means they look like they're smart, perhaps creative in some way, or with some kind of refined consciousness. I would like to make contact, but I am shy. I sit there quietly.

I just signed a year's lease on a house in this remote area where it looks as if I'll have minimal chance for developing any relationships. I think about going back to the house and cringe inside. I wonder if I stay here long enough if I'll eventually feel at home, and will think back to the present, when I feel so out of touch. I look out the tall glass window into the dark night and see the black street and dull green bushes. The inside of the café is also green, but glossy, with old-fashioned ornate moldings.

There's a woman in the café sitting by herself, reading. We make fleeting eye contact a few times – I wonder if I should try to talk with her. While I'm getting a coffee at the counter, she gets up and walks over to pick up a napkin. She's taller than me. I don't feel attracted to her physically now that I can see her body better, although I thought she had a pleasant face when she was sitting. I don't go over to her. Later, I wonder if she got up to show me she was taller than me.

I move to a new seat at the counter along the wall. Another woman comes over with her coffee, perching on a stool nearby. She's middle-aged, dressed stylishly, but doesn't have the magnetic charge to attract me. She's wearing tinted glasses, and I'm also uncomfortable not being able to see her eyes. I don't say anything to her either. I'm looking for a sexual connection.

FAT

I told the psychic:
When I held Rachel, she felt large, obese, even though she actually has a thin, nicely shaped figure.

The psychic told me:
It's because she was fat when she was your mother, a few lifetimes ago in Old Testament times when you both were Jews. She was grasping and clinging and tried to mold you to her expectations. You didn't want to get too close because of her clinging. You went away. You loved her but you were also inharmonious. Because you didn't resolve the situation in that life, the general type of woman you attract now wants to lean, cling, and drain your energy. You resist, and are accused of being non-generous. Open your heart to the woman inside to go past this.

I told the psychic:
It's true. Our main issue is that I won't support her. She's resentful, as if she feels I owe her.

The psychic told me:
Your next and previous life was around 700 A.D. as a North American Indian. I see you strong, teaching the young who want your approval. I see you as a chief, wanting to cry on the inside, but keeping a strong front.

I told the psychic:
It feels right. It feels as if my parents were part of my tribe from that period, maybe even my children. They always gave me complete freedom and respect as a child, as if they were in awe of me. My father was an outdoorsman, and belonged to a hunting and fishing club of fifteen or so members who called themselves *The Nomads*. I grew up with a natural affinity for boats and the water. I always felt I was reconnecting to my tribe and finishing karma when I lived on Martha's Vineyard in the seventies.

The psychic told me:
In an earlier life, I see you involved as an authority with religion on the earth plane. You were judgmental and harsh. Your Saturn sternness comes from this period. An important part of your present work is to overcome rigidity by cultivating your feeling and intuition.

I told the psychic:
I feel as if I've been doing that with my focus on creating and being an artist, even though it's opened me to a lot of pain.

The psychic told me:
Yes. And being a psychotherapist for you is the chance to payback for the harshness.

PHILOSOPHER

I was talking to the old philosopher
We met over breakfast
I tried to understand what he had learned
But he just ate his food quietly.

He was covered in a hand-made quilt
As he sat, thinking
What can we know?
What can we do?

Changed my job
Got tired thinking of security
Parachuting into unknown territory.

Fascination arises when the unconscious xxxxxx xxx xxxxx
the disturbing – the first step to xxx xxxx xxxxxxx xx xxxxx.

Stream of consciousness: Thought's dictation, independent of esthetic or moral preoccupation.

The association of two or more alien objects or elements on a plane alien to both is the most potent ignition of poetry.

Chance gives depth to a work of art, e.g., things arranged by chance.

COMMUNE

It's morning in a spiritual commune. Everyone is just waking up. They are all sleeping in a large room, on mattresses on the floor.

Near a window, a young woman sits with her breasts exposed. They look unique and beautiful in the sunlight. Brad can't resist staring, becoming aroused. He nudges into the side of his lover who's in bed with him. She reaches over and grabs his cock and then pulls him over and puts her mouth around it. They are ecstatic.

They get interrupted by a commotion across the room. Another couple was discovered having sex, which is against the rules of the commune. Several people indignantly accuse the guilty man. The confrontation becomes violent. One woman, a leader, shouts to cut off his dick.

Brad is greatly upset. He feels he should come to the defense of the accused man, but he's afraid for himself. Instead, he slips out the back door and runs for a phone to call the police. He hopes they can come before it's too late.

PHOTOGRAPHY

Russell went into the city last night to an opening and was surprised to see David there. Russell knew the opening was for three photographers including David, but he never expected him to attend, first, because this is San Francisco and David lives in New York, and second, he never thought David would mingle with the public, being a superstar. But there he was, standing in the middle of a small group, talking with them as if they were old friends. People were telling him things, and he appeared to be listening.

The opening itself was packed – it was a sensational event. Russell knew he had to go over to say something to him, but he didn't know what. He became nervous; he turned to stone. He couldn't imagine gathering the energy to converse with him. David seemed emotionally open, charismatic, maybe even more evolved. Russell couldn't take his eyes off him.

Russell's reaction was probably unlike that of most people there since David was such a powerful artistic influence on him, being largely responsible for changing the course of his musical expression in the eighties. It's hard to avoid hero worship when someone influences you so much. Russell felt in awe of him, of his success. He couldn't avoid identifying with him because they even looked similar. They are about the same age, sharing the same kinds of aging signs, and were probably the two oldest people there – it seemed everyone else was young. Both have dark hair, combed back, and both have a dark look. Both were wearing all black.

The identification twisted itself into comparison. David's experienced recognition and success as an artist; he's done what Russell wants most to do. All his feelings of never having made it big came up. The pain of failure and envy became acute. Finally, Russell dragged himself over to exchange a few sentences:

"Hi David, I just had to come over and say hello. (shake hands) I've been a fan since *Buildings and Food*."
"*Buildings and Food!* That sounds kind of cryptic." (laugh)
"Yeah. (laugh) I wanted to thank you for being such an important influence in my life – I'm a musician too. And it's great to see you doing this new stuff."
"Yes, and there's more on the way."

That was about it – someone else barged over and they had run out of conversation anyway. Of course, Russell felt as if he knew David and was shocked when David obviously didn't know him, even though he was cordial. The whole occasion was really one of going into shock. It was made even more disorienting and bizarre when a gay guy who knew Russell's name came over to hit on him. Russell had no idea where he had learned his name, and the man wouldn't or couldn't say. Russell thought perhaps he had seen his picture in his book; he didn't remember ever meeting him.

At that point, Russell was ready to leave. With feelings of futility, confusion, and loneliness he walked out of the gallery to his car and drove home.

LOCKER ROOM

When male students go to the gym for their athletics period, they see a sign saying the locker room has become co-ed. They are not sure what this is supposed to mean. Does it mean men and women will rotate using the facilities, or that they will be changing clothes and showering together from now on?

As they get undressed in the locker room they nervously look around, but see only guys changing. However, they soon notice a young woman with a trim perky body, completely naked, standing in front of her open locker, arranging her things on the bench. They carefully, instantly take note of her. They each try to decide how to act. Some realize it would be improper to stare, and so try not to, but most are unable to relax. Afterwards, they continue to be disturbed by the event.

GAS

I'm looking to re-locate. I've been in New York City for the past 20 years and I'm fed up with it. However, I'm unable to find another area where I feel at home.

I'm driving with some friends in New York State, about an hour north of the city. We are wandering aimlessly, just exploring. As we enter a little town, we see an industrial loft building with a "for rent live-in ok" sign. The building is unlocked so we go inside. It's three stories, all vacant. The open loft spaces are 40 feet square with high ceilings, windows all around, painted white. Excellent light. Nice wooden floors, maple. A positive, uplifting vibration noticeably fills the space. Outside the windows there's grass, trees, a brook across the field, and only a few other buildings close by. It's summer, so everything is warm, blooming, fertile.

One of my friends reminds me that if I take the place, I won't really be out in the country, which was my fantasy, but still in a town, even though it's a small town. I reply I don't care about that — there's enough woods here to satisfy me. I decide to take the third floor, without knowing anything else about the area, who might occupy the other spaces, the potential for community, etc.

We start to drive back to the city. We are in my parents' new Cadillac, which I borrowed for the trip even though I basically hate the car because of its pretentiousness. I'm driving. I pull into a self-service gas station to fill up. I go to put the gas nozzle into the Cadillac's tank, but I am unable to do so. There's a flexible metal hose, three feet long, sticking up out of the car in the back under the trunk where the tank input should be, like a grotesque tail. I try inserting the nozzle into the end of the hose, but that doesn't work – gas runs all over the ground. I get impatient and furious at not understanding how to even put gas in the fucking car, having to get out the instruction manual to figure this out, the ridiculous advancing of technology to nowhere except the destruction of the human spirit, and probably having to tell my parents about the problem.

At that point, one of the attendants at the station notices my quandary and comes over. He pulls the metal hose out of the car's gas input, puts it in the trunk, and fills the tank normally. He's quite pleasant. We all thank him, and go on our way.

TWO 100'S

I am with a friend I don't recognize who has a very short haircut. He has just done something for which he has received a grade of two 100's, an exceptionally high mark. He is not a student, but some kind of teacher, and not normally seeking inordinate recognition. Now, however, he wants to be fussed over, feeling he has achieved something. I massage him and praise him. We are on my living room couch. His clothes come off. He has an erection, which I want to grab and caress, but don't. His body is beautiful, but there's something that doesn't attract me totally in a sexual way.

BREAKFAST

It's morning in a small European country town. I'm walking about, searching for a place to have breakfast. I enter a warm-looking restaurant. Inside, there are dark heavy wooden beams on the walls and ceiling interspersed with white plaster. A pretty young woman with long brown hair is sitting at a thick wooden table. I'm attracted to her, but I'm not confident enough to try to talk with her. I sit at a nearby table, observing her discreetly. She's dressed in an old-fashioned billowy, flowery dress with long sleeves and a straw bonnet. She appears refined, gentle. Another woman joins her. The second woman is older, with gray hair. They talk animatedly; I am able to hear bits of the conversation. They seem to be discussing feelings in a clinical way, as if they might be psychologists.

But soon, the first woman, the one I'm attracted to, begins to change. Her face loses its charm. Hair appears on her cheeks, not thick like the beard of a man, but sparse and curly. Her manner, which had been so sweet, becomes garrulous. I am repulsed, but fascinated. After a while the older woman leaves. Turning my chair so I am at her side, I speak to her:

"Hello, could we talk for a minute?"
"No, I don't think so," she replies.
"I think you would find it interesting."
"Why is that?"
"Because I'm from a different time. What year is it here?"
"1948."

When I hear this, I become emotional. I feel as if I have finally achieved a difficult, long-sought goal, although it now seems odd that time travel would mean so much to me. I sense a welling-up from a deep, hidden place – it's a strong, physical feeling shaking my body. Tears come. I snap back to the present.

SENSITIVE

They look like a bunch of ordinary people, but they can produce a work of magic. I'm with my father and my unidentified girlfriend at a movie lot down at the shore. We are staying at my parents' house. I want to linger around to watch the crew as they work, to see how the magic is made. My father doesn't understand this and wants to go. I become enraged, screaming at him, trying to explain to him. I'm furious at his lack of sensitivity to the magic and doubly furious at having to justify such delicate things. Am I reacting to myself? Does the lack of sensitivity come from inside me? Do I reject the insensitivity inside and project it onto my father, rejecting him? Do I identify with the sensitive and think it makes me better?

Back at the house, music coming from outside disturbs me. It invades my privacy and makes me mad. It makes it harder to concentrate. The music stops.

What about Eve's insensitivity? She has the same aspect in her chart as in my father's – Moon opposite Saturn. I was horrified about her lack of receptivity when we last spoke. It's always the same – I'm supporting her. Is it the lack of support I give myself?

Later, I'm in my bedroom. I've been playing guitar and singing softly to myself, thinking I am alone when I see my mother leaning on the door frame outside the room. She's been listening. I'm enraged at her intrusion and scream at her to leave me the fuck alone.

PROTECT

    |||| <>   Object protect

G0t my new stick on my knee, don't you see
Clap when you are ready
There's two of us, and that's enough.

Protect this object

Clamshell smooth, heartspun smooth
Spendthrift smooth, extra smooth.

Get the best

Protect this object.

ARCHETYPES

The recognition of the collective shadow leads to the world of the *archetypes*. The archetypes exist in the same magical realm of which we have spoken earlier, on a psychic plane inside us and available to all of us. They are normally not conscious to us but instead influence us indirectly, by shaping the possibilities of our experience. When we enter the magical realm, we access the archetypes directly. In art, the archetypes manifest on the physical plane.

There are a few ways of understanding what an archetype is and does for us. First, an archetype may be seen as a kind of ideal, cosmic blueprint for relationship roles. For example, there is the archetype of the mother, the father, the lover, the warrior, the priest, even the artist. Each of these archetypal models contains the ideal qualities of that role. The archetypal mother is gentle, nurturing, warm, supportive, unconditionally loving. The archetypal father is protective, strong, dominant, guiding, conditionally loving. The archetypal lover is beautiful and sexual and contains modified qualities of the opposite sex archetypal parent. The archetypal warrior has courage and strength. The archetypal priest receives spiritual inspiration and guides devotion. The archetypal artist is innovative, rebellious, and challenging of society's conventions.

When we experience archetypal qualities in relationship to others, either in them or ourselves, we are usually encouraged and fulfilled. If we do not find these qualities, we tend to be disappointed and unfulfilled. However, this does not mean others are failures if they do not reflect archetypal qualities to us. Rather, it means *we are closed off to the recognition of those qualities within ourselves*. In this way, we contribute directly to our experience of the manifest world.

For example, if you experienced a difficult childhood with a parent who did not come close to the archetype, it means you are not clear enough within yourself to perceive the archetypal. You are blocking your inner male or female. Accepting this may be a difficult step, but it is part of the all-important taking of responsibility. As you *empower* yourself by taking responsibility, you begin the process of clearing the inner blocks that obscure your perception of both the shadow and the transcendental archetype.

Another and perhaps deeper way of understanding the archetypes is from the emotional viewpoint; we find there is a blueprint in place for our feeling experience. Moreover, the emotional blueprint occurs in *dualistic* form, as do also the archetypes for relationships; the positive and negative co-exist, side by side. Just as there is the possibility of great happiness in being with a loved one, there is the possibility of great sadness in loneliness. Just as the mother can be unconditionally nurturing, she can be suffocating and engulfing. The two possibilities are formed together in the archetypal realm, like the two sides of a coin. The implications of the dualistic aspect of emotional experience are of tremendous consequence as we try to understand and heal our feeling selves.

We must realize each emotional experience is based on its dualistic complement, each could not exist without the other, and that we must allow a place in our awareness for *both* sides. We will be unable to experience any one side without some kind of acquaintance with the other. We will be fulfilled in accomplishment; we will be angry and frustrated in failure. We will be recognized in our expression; we will be unnoticed and ignored. We will be secure; we will be afraid. We will love and we will hate.

In the mature handling of the dualistic experience, we cultivate a sense of equanimity in the face of each side. Our attachment to the positive loosens; our resistance to the negative eases up. Since we understand that each depends on the other for its existence, we see the futility in mindlessly and compulsively chasing after the "positive" in order to avoid the "negative." Such activity only builds the suppressed negative, which will eventually rebound upon us. Negative feelings must be accepted and experienced – they cannot be compensated for by more of the positive.

As we hold ourselves in this position of equanimity regarding the positive and negative, we find our entire experience changes. It does not mean we must spend half our time enduring the pain of the negative; rather, when we bring both sides into balance, we have a basically positive experience of the entire dualistic dynamic, and ultimately transcend the issue in question; we have *integrated* the negative. We are no longer caught up in the vicious dualistic circle. We emerge onto a new, higher plane of experience and fulfillment not dependent upon satisfaction of dualistic desire. But before we reach that point, in order to get into balance, we need to go through the suppressed negative.

Many of us are in the position of seemingly never being able to realize what we want most, whether this concerns a relationship, raising a family, getting the recognition we want, feeling financially secure, and so on. Wherever you are most frustrated is where you need to work; it is the suppressed negativity within that holds you back. Until it is cleared, consciously and deliberately, it is not likely you will find meaningful fulfillment. This suppressed negativity manifests as painful feelings. When you start working on the feeling level, you begin the process of lasting change, and in order to work on the feelings, you must open to them.

In opening to feelings, we find that the basis of much of the emotional chaos we undergo is not the "negative" feeling itself, but our *resistance* to the negative. The resistance itself creates pain and compounds the original feeling. The resistance often leads to counter-productive escapism. As we move past all forms of resistance, we find feelings clear quickly and effortlessly through being fully engaged.

As we investigate the emotional archetypes inside ourselves further, we notice they represent the *extremes* of experience. Just as role archetypes represent the ideal, so do emotional archetypes represent the ideal dualistic manifestation of both joy and suffering. We don't normally resist the positive side of each dualism; we readily embrace love, success, health, or praise unless our inner blocking interferes. But when we glimpse the negative poles of the archetypes, we are tempted to run. The negative poles consist of tremendous suffering and pain – essentially the worst (or highest) you can imagine, because when you imagine, you enter the magical realm, the home of the archetypes.

This is where the artist steps in. The artist, in creating, surrenders to the guidance of the artist archetype. In doing so, the work is taken out of her or his hands. Although the artist may start with a personal theme that yearns to manifest, soon the archetypal emerges if the artist knows how to allow it. The archetypal may appear in the form of the artist's personal themes, but there is no mistaking the power of the archetype; we are moved because we recognize its universality. In a way, the recognition of the archetype becomes a bridge between the personal experience of the artist and our own personal experience. We see, if we are willing, that the intense pain depicted in the art, the violence, the loneliness, the desperation, the depression unquestionably exists inside us, that *it has to be* part of us as we are members of the human collective. And if we are brave, we accept what we see, knowing acceptance is the first step to integration and transcendence. If we can make this leap, we start to use the art for our healing.

Although great art must contain both the positive to inspire us and the negative to enlighten us, artists are often moved to portray negative archetypes more than positive, as I have presented in this book. This is because the artist sees it is the negative that needs to be recognized most; this is where our rejection and resistance lies; this is what needs to be brought to light. Often artists are dismayed by the tremendous hypocrisy surrounding these issues, evidenced when we condemn others for qualities common to us all. Artists may also be preoccupied with dark issues because their experience in uncovering negative archetypes within themselves has been so important for their own growth, and they desire to share their discoveries, as best as can be accepted by their audience. Or, they may simply be compelled by the part of the artist archetype that needs to challenge, upset, reform, and bring to light those hidden and denied parts of the collective that cause so much pain by being suppressed from the mass consciousness.

This is the primary role of the artist in society – to bring forth the new, evolving consciousness; to move us in ways that make us unable to remain unaware of the neglected shadow; to facilitate the dawning of higher awareness that must include acceptance of the unwanted lower. As we open to meet the challenge, we open to evolution and fulfillment.

BUS

I'm on my way to work, waiting at the bus stop with others. I'm a counselor. I just moved to England for six months on an exchange program. The bus pulls in, and as I'm standing in line to get on, I'm astounded to see my old guru sitting behind the wheel. He's on the right-hand side of the vehicle, in the small driver's compartment they have on the buses in London. He's collecting fare and checking tickets. He's dressed in a flowing white robe with beads. His long hair, almost shoulder length, has grayed more since I saw him last – I realize it's been almost ten years. I immediately notice he's doing the bus driver's job with the same radiant poise and equanimity he always displayed whenever I saw him or heard him speak at the ashram. I spontaneously and poignantly feel the same attraction to his luminous energy I've always felt.

At the same time, I am embarrassed about accidentally discovering him in his new life. I feel he will be humiliated to be found doing this menial job after having been known as such a highly respected teacher. He hasn't seen me, so I sneak past him to the back of the bus, hiding behind the crowd. But then, I question my action. Was I really being considerate in avoiding him? Or was it just my own lack of ease and inclination to hide that I was experiencing? I realize I do not know what he feels.

Later, after work, I stop at the home of one of my clients for tea. She, her boyfriend and I sit talking. Her boyfriend mentions he is 36 years old, and asks her how old she is. I am surprised he doesn't know this information. She replies 32. He appears satisfied. However, I know from her records she is 42, and looks it. After having my attention drawn to her appearance, I start noticing her body. She looks ripe and sexy. I decide I will try to get her to sleep with me.

WRONG

Let me tell you what went wrong: There was never any good talk there anyway and some people didn't like each other. There were many who were trying to say what they thought the trouble was but they couldn't be listened to. A good feeling is never too much for a date, but how about a horse? Never mind, you don't know what I mean anyway. Ride that bicycle all around town. You look like a teen-ager the way you dress. City vibes always had something else to say but I guess I'll call it a day. Did I accomplish anything? It's not something you can point to, like a company, or a house. To many people it would be meaningless. Certainly not center-stage. The most important things anyway. Things as rewards are not important if you don't earn them.

HALLWAY

I'm lying in a hallway, sick. I'm in an institutional building, with other people who are sick. We are side by side on the floor, with heads against one of the walls, bodies perpendicular. It seems as though I've been here a long time.

I get tired of these surroundings and move outside, where there is a sidewalk with many people passing. I lie down in a pathway between the building and the sidewalk. Naked, face down in the dirt, caressing the earth, I glance up at the faces going by, but nobody looks at me. After a while, I roll myself tightly in a blanket with only my head sticking out, still lying on my front, facing the crowd. Then, having had enough of this, I resolve that I am well.

I go into a different building and find a party going on. I take a seat against the wall. Dave, someone I knew in high school, sits next to me. He appears not to recognize me, but mistakes me for a woman because I am covered with only my face showing. I liked Dave, but never saw any intellectuality in him to draw me into a friendship, even though he was a tremendous athlete and a hero. Now, he's trying to charm me, non-stop. I find this amusing. I enjoy his attention. I can't think of anything to say, but squirm around with a big smile on my face.

Soon, I leave Dave. I see a woman who interests me, so I go over to her. We talk, but lose each other in the crowd. I see another woman who attracts me. I go over to her and try to make her want me, but I don't want the first woman to know. The first woman, however, comes over to talk to us. It turns out they are friends and came to the party together. I tell them I haven't had any women in my life for a while, and now I can't decide between them.

PERFECT

I'm sitting in front of the computer at my mother's house, scanning the Internet. It's evening. My mother is about to go to bed.

She comes over to say good-night, wearing a tan terrycloth robe, and tells me I might want to look at the site for Michael Bolito, who she says is a famous painter. She goes to her bedroom.

I search the web, but all I find is over a thousand references to Spanish wine-making. I don't understand her suggestion.

She comes back out of the bedroom to see how I did, walking up behind me as I'm sitting in the chair. Her robe is open. I swivel around and without thinking, reach with my arms under the robe, around her naked body. I run my cheek between her full breasts, down against her stomach, and against her brown pubic hair. Her body is perfect. I am utterly, completely aroused. I realize I compare every woman to my perception of her.

OIL

My father has built a boat for me. We are out in the boat — it's a neat 18' outboard runabout with a cabin and two bunks. We are in the cockpit behind the cabin, trying to pour some engine oil from one container to another. He spills some oil on the gray floorboards. As I get down on my knees to wipe it up, he spills more. I become enraged because he's careless and is messing up my boat. I yell at him as loud as I can: stupid asshole.

SUICIDE CLUB

For Sam – a middle-aged writer – life keeps getting worse. He finds it difficult to get work, and those writing assignments he does manage to obtain don't really interest him and, he feels, are unimportant. As a result, the quality of his writing has drastically declined, leaving him even less likely to attract worthwhile possibilities. The downward spiral has far removed him from his previous career peaks, which included publishing a successful novel as a young man.

Life has become solitary and jagged without, it seems, possibility for meaningful relationship. He is easily provoked by small, everyday annoyances such as barking dogs and inconsiderate neighbors. Desperately, he goes to therapy. He drops in on various spiritual organizations. But nothing seems to work. He remains angry, frustrated, and depressed.

One day, while sitting aimlessly in a coffee-house where would-be authors congregate, Sam sees a mysterious classified ad in the paper for a *Suicide Club*. Curious, he goes to a meeting. He discovers the club supports those who wish to end their lives, and provides a philosophy to make them feel better about doing it. There are regular meetings in which members are prepared for the last step.

The actual act is done with all the participants lying on the floor. Each has an apparatus that injects a slow-acting poison into their system. Over the course of about a half hour, they become drowsy and finally drift off. There is no pain. The injector is a comb-like instrument with five teeth that prick the uppermost layer of the skin, allowing the poison to slowly enter from a tube running from the comb to a bottle hanging on a stand, like an intravenous setup. It is best applied in the abdominal area.

The first meeting Sam attends is strongly emotional for him and he feels an immediate resonance. With discontent and depression so prevalent today, many are secretly fascinated by the idea of ending their lives, and the meeting is well-attended, the discussion animated. People give convincing testimonies about how they can see no alternative but to take their life. Some of the testimonies are on videotape – those who have successfully gone on.

The philosophy of self-termination is explained: Today's world is in absolute chaos. Love – which alone gives meaning to life – cannot exist; anytime it attempts to appear it is ruthlessly trampled by the forces of self-interest and hatred that ultimately rule each of us. There can be no god who would allow such conditions to continue, or if there is a god somewhere, there is at least no question that god is unconcerned about us. Actualizing the option of taking one's life is the only real choice for a person of integrity – the only genuine statement that can be made in this hopeless world – it's the statement that I will not take this indignity any longer and I'm going to do something final about it.

Others voice the opposing view: Man has free-will, and is only experiencing the results of unwise choices made in the past, either by the collective as a whole or the reincarnating individual. Yes, life is hard, but we are to face the challenge and develop our capacity to love using the obstacles as incentives; this is how we grow. Taking one's life is a mortal sin, or bad karma, that must be worked off in another life. And after you do it, you only find yourself in the next world, similar to this one with the same problems, only more severe, because you didn't take the opportunity to resolve them that the earth life offers.

Being an intellectual, Sam finds the arguments interesting, but ironically, because of his disillusionment with his career, he has learned to not trust the intellect, a notion he has found to be reinforced by most Eastern philosophies. He finds himself leaning in the direction of his gut feelings, which consist of intense weariness and the simple desire for oblivion.

But there is an unexpected development. Without his seeking it, a romantic interest begins with another female member of the club. She and Sam start to notice each other. Under different circumstances, Sam would have welcomed the opportunity, but now he is hostile towards her, avoiding her, defending against the attraction he feels, cynically thinking he will never find love, and the devil is tempting him to stay alive only because it is becoming more and more apparent to him that he is going to go through with it. But she can sense an attraction. Even though they don't speak at any of the meetings, her attitude towards him is consistently open and compassionate. All feelings in her have been repressed, but she can still respond to the opportunity of caring about someone else, if not herself, for whom she has given up hope.

The time finally comes when Sam feels he is ready to go ahead. He has gone through the preparation, and will now take part in the final phase with seven other candidates. They meet in the evening at the apartment the club rents. After some ritual and meditation, all the candidates lie down on the rug. Each has two other club members to guide them through the process – comforting them, assuring them, holding them. The lights are dim, ethereal music is softly playing, the atmosphere is warm and loving, as if something wonderful is about to happen.

Sam applies the comb to his stomach and starts to feel the initial effects of the poison entering his system. He drifts away, letting go. However, after a short while he becomes distressed. He remembers he has not prepared his will, and in spite of his depressed indifference to all mundane matters that has kept him from addressing this detail, he is stricken by guilt that he will inflict his aged parents with the task of settling his estate, which will confuse and upset them even more. Not having anyone in his life, he decides, on the moment, to leave all his money to the Author's Guild, an idea he has been entertaining but has not yet acted on. He removes the comb and excuses himself, stumbling out of the room, intending to go to his apartment to sign a simple statement he will leave on his desk where it will be found.

However, it has snowed in the city while he has been in the room with the group, and in his drugged condition he is unable to walk through it to get home. It is now late at night, and seeing a 24-hour diner down the street, he goes inside. Despondently, he sits there with a cup of coffee, not knowing what to do next. Soon, the woman with whom Sam has had the secret attraction comes into the diner and sits down at a table on the other side of the room. She was also taking part in the evening. She is the only person in his life who might be able to get through to him.

Sam walks to the center of the diner and stands there, right in front of the chrome and glass door, thinking about trying to go outside again. She comes over. She tells him she couldn't go through with it. He says he's not sure, he's not free of it yet. It's the first time they have spoken. They don't know what to do or say next. Sam is still wearing the pajama-like outfit from the meeting under his coat. She playfully, cautiously, asks him what he's wearing under it. Nothing, he replies. Let's see, she says, tugging at the elastic around his waist with her finger and making a fake attempt to peek down his trousers. Sam is tickled. No, he says, laughing and pulling away. She looks at him with a beautiful, saving smile on her face. It makes him smile. The depression has been broken. Sam is clear of danger. He has been saved by love. Together, they save each other.

DUCKS

I was making controlled, exact marks on the paper, trying to represent eyes. It felt like I was struggling. I let go into a scribble, moving the pencil in wide loops and circles with no particular image in mind, surrendering to the guidance of the unconscious. In the loops, a woman's figure started to appear. I filled in consciously some body parts, and saw the direction was from the source. I switched to painting. I was in a high energy place – in touch with the source – anything I put down had the magic. I started another painting where the guidance took over completely. I literally watched as the force quickly formed the images. And the images were very unsquare – no neatness, no right angles, no balance in the picture – but that was part of the tremendous expression of life and power. I drew ducks – starting at the bottom – putting them one on top of the other on the right side of the paper. I knew when it was finished. I did another. It came quickly – in under a minute – just a splash of color, but the power was there. I relaxed into a huge catharsis, weeping.

RELEASE

Travels in the astral: I saw Max last night. We were in a large room with heavy timber beams on the ceiling and planks on the floor, dimly lit by a yellow glow. He was the same age as when I knew him in college. He was a Quaker and a very good-looking kid. It turns out he was putting his good looks to use by sleeping around with a lot of women. None of the rest of us knew about it – I guess he wanted to maintain his Quaker image. One woman, becoming attached to Max, was deeply hurt. I could see her hanging around his neck, attached in spirit form with a gruesome wound in her chest, as if she had been impaled with a spike.

Max wanted me to heal him so I tried to release the spirit, who I felt was dangerous to both him and me. I started circling him in my astral form while speaking to the spirit, telling it how much it was loved and missed by its conscious self. I circled in a motionless, standing but crouched position, continuously facing him, as if I were a figure on a revolving carousel with him on the stationary floor in the center. All of our forms seemed lit from within, bright against the darkness of the room. The spirit released itself and disappeared.

Max wanted to sleep now, so he laid down on the floor under a white canvas cover. I laid down also, a short distance from him, but he kept shifting around, coming closer and closer to me, making me nervous. I started vibrating in my astral body again to protect myself, getting up and moving away.

Then my attention was drawn across the room. Another girlfriend of Max's had appeared, this time real in the flesh. She was wearing a thin, transparent, light blue negligee, through which her pale white body was visible. She was leaning forward slightly, hands on hips, rocking so her breasts swung up and down. They were medium-large, droopy. She came over to me and became affectionate. She put her mouth on my ear, darting her tongue in and out incredibly quickly. I put my arm around her bare waist and could feel her vibration. She was pulsating, cellular, her pelvis shaking in surreal intensity. The realness was staggering. Then I saw Max watching us from under his cover.

NATURAL HISTORY

Relativity, and the discontinuance of Newtonian physics, applies to the inner as well as the outer world. A new, irrational order, it's laws, processes, contents are unimaginable.

Modern art seeks to give visible form to the life behind things, the secret pattern of things.

Writing is talking about the feeling; music is the feeling.

ZOMBIE

Jimmy's mother has just returned from the hospital where she has had an operation. They are standing in the kitchen of their old house. She looks renewed, much younger and beautiful. She is wearing a low-cut dark blue-green lacy dress. She holds him close and tells him he is the love and center of her life. He is naked. He is embarrassed at her disclosure and his nakedness.

Then, some of her friends arrive. She apparently wants them to see him naked but this embarrasses him more, so he runs up the stairs to his room and locks the door. The people follow him up the stairs and try to push into the room. While he's busy holding the door locked, a few of them break through the wall around a corner where he can't see. Soon they are walking in the room. He feels invaded. He grabs a stick that has short pieces of flat metal wire sticking out on the end and starts hitting them in the face with it, but it doesn't affect them. They are walking zombie-like, inspecting the room, discussing whether to buy it. He grabs a heavier wooden clothes pole out of the closet. He discovers that if he hits them twice in the head with the pole, swinging as hard as he can, they will fall down. He continues to hit them.

TV

My friend Phil has just moved into a new apartment in Philadelphia and has asked me to help him carry in a large TV. I drive into the city and park a short distance from his place, in what seems to be a safe area. When I get to his building, I see he's already got the TV out on the front lawn. He's waiting for me, along with his girlfriend and a woman friend of hers. The four of us talk for a bit before getting down to the business at hand.

Phil has made a carrier for the TV, which consists of two long poles with boards nailed across them. The carrier is a dark bluish-gray color. We put the TV on the boards, lift the poles onto our shoulders, and start walking towards the building, with me in front and him behind. Just as we get to the stairs, Phil tells me to hold it a minute; he remembers he has to take a leak. He lets go of his end of the carrier but to my amazement, it doesn't fall. I continue to hold my end, watching him. Phil turns to his side, opens his pants and starts to piss right there on the grass, in front of us all, without the slightest sense of indecency or self-consciousness. The women also don't seem to find anything unusual in Phil's behavior. Not only that, but he lets loose a tremendous flow of liquid, as if he had turned on a hose – it shoots out about six feet onto the lawn. My astonishment and judgmentalism are compounded by my envy, since I am currently having prostate trouble and can't pee so well. Done, Phil goes back to his end of the carrier, still suspended. We go up the stairs to the apartment with no further complications. We talk some more, and then I leave.

When I get back to my car, I find the neighborhood has changed in the short time I have been away. It has become deserted, seedy, dangerous-looking. Grass has grown tall, garbage and graffiti are scattered about. I see a threatening-looking man walking on the sidewalk near my car. I wait until he passes before I go over to the car. As I get to the car, an old VW bug in top condition, I see it has been broken into. The seats and dashboard have been removed.

TALK

I spoke with Jill yesterday. She talked for a while about her work, then I tried to explain my problem with women not being good listeners for me, but me always doing that for them. I asked her if they are insensitive or just impolite or is it something in me?

She said women are emotionally all over the place and look for a man who is stable to hang on to. They are in pain and not aware of what they are doing. They have unresolved feelings they attempt to fix by talking. Not many men will talk about feelings. The man usually wants to talk about himself, so when they find a man who can listen, they go bananas.

We clarified that there is an energy support the listener gives the talker. In a good conversation, both people will listen and talk, and both come away feeling heard and supported. In a one-sided conversation, one person is drained. I told Jill that was sometimes my experience with her. She understood and didn't get upset. She mentioned some other interesting things, such as when she rejects part of herself in a relationship she becomes addicted to the other person to fill that part in order to feel whole.

I told her about the woman I just met. I liked her because she has the drive to be an artist. I get attracted to that in women. I have never been with a woman like that – maybe it's something I wouldn't be comfortable with when I had it, but now it seems like what I want. I talked a lot with the new woman and was excited at being heard for once. I may have talked too much and perhaps intimidated or took advantage of her. She might have felt run over the way I do with many women, feeling they are selfish.

FIND OUT

verse 1
Well I've got to admit, this is easier than working. The backward feelings I get, I push them down into the ocean. The rewards are so great, the many people that I'm helping. Make my day so complete, like a vacation with advancement. All I do is

chorus
 Find out, if the person is breathing
 Point out, the important things that he's seeing
 Try to, persuade him into believing
 Make sure, he understands the full meaning

verse 2
Today I'm feeling great, sold a two-family to a young couple. They're going to paint it and fix it up themselves. Invest in it throughout the years. Let the income pay off the mortgage and then give it to the kids. I just

chorus
 Find out, if the person is breathing
 Point out, the important things that he's seeing
 Try to, persuade him into believing
 Make sure, he understands the full meaning

verse 3
Had a bad day today. Showed a bunch of places to a man from Alabama. Seemed like a nice person, but turned out to be an escaped convict. Selling real estate is not always easy, but I try to look on the bright side. I

chorus
  Find out, if the person is breathing
  Point out, the important things that he's seeing
  Try to, persuade him into believing
  Make sure, he understands the full meaning

fade out
This is it   the lawn   the front porch
the clothes closet   the fireplace
the kitchen   the dishwasher   the backyard
master bedroom   with bathroom   the air conditioner
the school's down the street   the neighbors are quiet

note: verses and fade out to be spoken; choruses

  to be sung – make up your own melody

REASON

Tell me the reason I can't go out tonight. Think it over. Bush by the road, strawberry in the hay. Little babies by the house. I don't want to die. Cyclotron sister, cyclotree, run in circles when you're free. Make another stand, far from the crowd. Live a terrible part of the unknown tragedy. Zip the shade. Pull on the rear portion. Let me sink to the level I forgot. Never, never tell the thing you need. Put something on me, I'm cold. Show me the best part now. Give me a reason to laugh, but don't tell me any jokes. Put down the hammer. Pull up the forest. I think she is coming. Too soon. Say what you need. Is the other arrangement better? I say don't put it on. You look good, but don't let me hear. Cyclostand, the weather makes it hard, but don't mind the pigs on the road. I find

NEXT LIFE

What would it take to make me come back again? They say you don't return except by choice.

So, there I am, I've passed over into the next life, and about five centuries Earth time have gone by. It's been wonderful, but now I'm getting restless, and some work needs to be done again. But I don't have to go back unless I want to, unless something is promised me that I want to have. What would that be? If I could be David Bowie, would I take it? Or is it something much simpler?

It's dream-time,
a fire-fly world,
multi-dimensional softness
to caress your soul.
You rest easy,
being held.

Aeons pass,
but it's all here now.
Then, tender machinery
nudges you.
Desire, the desire,
your old companion, desire,
smiles at you again, and you
remember

There's something you need to do.

WRESTLING

Al goes to a lecture on one of his favorite sports, collegiate-style wrestling. He listens attentively and after the lecture, goes up to the speaker and asks him if there's anyplace where they could wrestle now. The speaker says he doesn't actually do that anymore because it's too hard on his body; instead, he does *putzen*, a type of wrestling where opponents grasp each other only on the arms and try to throw each other to the mat. Al makes a date to drop in on the speaker's wrestling group to try this.

Al is the antithesis of me. I am reclusive – I want to be in a quiet place. Al lives where the action is – right on the Pacific Coast Highway. Al races his motorcycle down the highway and drives his four-wheeler over other cars. His image personifies the rebel, the independent, the fighter.

I see that my own life is incredibly dull and I need to identify with him. I suck energy from him.

MEETING

A friend of mine has a house in Saratoga Springs. We go up for a weekend. On the first evening, a neighbor of his serves us dinner in the house. My friend mentions he pays the neighbor six dollars for each dinner. The neighbor seems familiar to me. After a while, I recognize him as Michael, someone I knew many years ago. I'm surprised his appearance has not changed much. He shows no sign of recognizing me, and I'm not sure if I want to acknowledge him. It seems awkward if not embarrassing to have discovered him in this servile role, but finally we speak.

It's the Christmas season, and Michael comes back later that evening with a present for me. I'm reluctant to accept the gift because it looks as if he's making a play for me. We put off the gift dilemma until later.

We all go to a small restaurant-club owned by Michael. The interior is elegant – entirely gold with fantastically designed sculpture and fixtures. It's early, we are the only ones there. We sit at a table. I become excited about asking him if he happens to know the whereabouts of my old girlfriend Johnna, who was a close friend of his, but with whom I have lost contact. However, he becomes busy and I am unable to ask.

SERIOUS

Why do you remind yourself of him, the person you hate?

A soul locked in a body.

Your anger is killing us.

We can't stop what's coming.

You say I keep you from being yourself.

All I try to do is help.

I film you during sex.

Death is just the other side.

Why are you so afraid of poverty?

You don't listen to me / I can't express myself.

If you're strong enough.

Am I doing this to get somewhere?

You may be in serious trouble.

I think I'm sitting here quietly enjoying myself, but behind it I'm driven.

MOON AND WALKING

In astrology, the moon represents the mysterious and mystical; the dreamworld; the feminine; the realm of feeling including intuition, mood, and emotion; the magical. Herein lies the domain of the subconscious. When we invoke the magical, we enter the diffuse consciousness of the moon. Our sense of ego is lessened; we merge with soft images. We glimpse the noble, powerful, and timeless archetypal essences behind the earth-time manifestations of thought and form. We surrender to the magnetic pull of the dark, engulfing womb of creation. We lie there, balanced delicately, poised in stillness, watching as elemental forces rush through us into full consciousness, clothed in the personal, that can be apprehended and communicated.

"Walking" to me is a metaphor for our mundane experience. We keep on walkin' through life's dramas, often with resistance, but sometimes with acceptance and grace. If we have no connection to the moon, our walking can easily become stagnant and dreary. We are without magic, without contact to any source of replenishment. We walk only to arrive, we do not celebrate in our walking. To be in balance is to be not only in the walking, but to be in rapport with the moon. Then, we are somewhere between the moon and the walking, bringing each to balance the other, because neither by itself would be entirely beneficial. If we existed solely in the moon, we would be susceptible to being swept away by the elemental forces of the archetypes; we need the walking to ground us. In practical terms, art itself – the manifestation of feeling in form – is that place between the moon and the walking.

In the work I have presented here, there are many images of the normally hidden side of human experience. As each of these images appeared to me, I was consistently moved by the power it seemed to hold. Sometimes the images represented feelings high and glorious, but more often they are dark and disturbing. The darkness predominates because it is what has been repressed in us all; it is what needs to be uncovered for us to come into balance. Each dark image always seemed to portray perfectly a certain side of myself, but to portray it extended to the extreme; otherwise, it would not contain the power. What this means to me is that I contacted the perfect, ideal representation of the negative inside myself – the most painful, the most violent, the most driven, the most selfish, the most lonely – in other words, the negative archetype.

Why has this been of any benefit? By opening to and experiencing the archetypes inwardly and consciously, through the images of the stories, I have traveled beyond the personal into the universal, to the collective; I have realized, and trusted, that these feelings and forces are common to us all; my sense of self has expanded. Encouraged by this, it has been easier for me to move into acceptance of the feelings and away from resistance. I have enabled my personal process of reclaiming, of integrating those parts of myself previously suppressed. Most importantly, I have felt the healing power of the archetypes. Even, and possibly especially with regard to the "negative" archetypal feelings, is the healing power accessed.

How can this be of benefit to you, the reader? You can enter into the exact same process by opening to the work contained here or any other art that resonates with you, letting it bring forth your own personal feelings, as catalyzed by the art. Or, possibly you may be inspired enough to take it one step further and create your own art, applying the principles we have discussed. What's important is to open to your own feelings through the art, especially the negative ones of the shadow.

When we open to the negative feeling inwardly, something magical happens that can't be explained in scientific or logical terms. We receive the influx of energy we were blocking; the negative feeling itself becomes released into awareness, satisfied and dissolved; our sense of wholeness expands. This is how I would urge you to look at the excursion we have been taking. We have traveled into places that perhaps have not always been comfortable; however, I trust you have developed an appreciation for the growth that can come from opening to those dark places.

Art is a source of replenishment. When we recognize the archetypal forces that come through in the art, we contact the source within. The archetypes are alive with infinite cosmic force that will, with its own intelligence, enter our personal self and heal as is needed, whether on the physical or emotional level.

All through history, we see the inclusion of art in the mystical and spiritual: The dance, music, and images of the shaman; the drama of ancient mythologies; the symbolism and music of the religious; the mandalas of the contemplative East. In modern times, we see that we are drawn instinctively to powerful presentations in film, music, and literature to give us the experience of communion with the mystical, magical unconscious. We can't live without the connection to the magical realm; art takes us there.

This does not mean that we must necessarily be a producer of art. The primary capacity required to fruitfully engage art is to be able to receive: To be able to open to the experience that is before us; to be sensitive enough to receive the power from the archetypes; to be able to be moved. It is in the receiving that we are replenished.

Replenishment is one of the characteristics of the magical realm. Here, we are closer to the ultimate source of creative power and can feel it more directly. This power flows through the various planes of unmanifest creation and appears to us as emanating from the magical realm, the next higher level in our consciousness development. This level is also referred to as the astral plane in mystical vocabulary.

The astral plane is primarily emotional. We have seen, however, that the magical, or astral, realm contains all kinds of experiences and feelings. Some of these are challenging for us; we have often blocked ourselves off from awareness of them because of our fear of them. If we can approach these experiences, we open ourselves to the source of replenishment, healing, and growth.

Regarding "interpretation" of the pieces, I would again remind you that I encourage you to find your own meanings as reflections of the inner — what's important is what you can bring alive from and for yourself. There may be found multiple layers of symbolism and feeling in substantial art that will correspond to layers within the artist's psyche, but it is not necessary or even possible for the viewer to decipher this. Rather, just assume the complexity and subtlety contained in the art will add to the potential depth of your experience as it acts on you.

The stories may be grouped by types of inner experience; for example, there are the areas of fear and insecurity, sexual craving, the struggle for recognition and achievement, parental dynamics, blocked creativity, romance and relationship dilemmas. Although all the pieces are images of myself, at times I have chosen to create personalities who consistently reflect certain issues. Thus, Frank is the personality preoccupied with fear issues; Jimmy has parental dependency issues; Russell is the frustrated artist, and so on. Personalizing inner voices in this way helps to break the identification with the feelings they represent, which is necessary for successful processing.

If you cannot relate to any of the feelings presented in this work, it may be you are still unconsciously coming from the left-brain. You may be looking for meaning outside yourself instead of experiencing from within, directly through the right-brain – the intuitive, magical self. Or it may simply be that now is not the time for you to be involved with deep, inner-directed psychological work. It may be more important for you at this point in your personal cycles to focus your energy outward. However, it is probably safe to assume that at some period of your life you will discover landscapes within that correspond to those painted here. The archetypes, remember, are ideal representations of the *collective unconscious* – both the ideal positive and the ideal negative contained within *all* of us – that's why they are called archetypes. There is no question they are in you, although their formation will be personal.

If we are to evolve as humans on our journey to spirit, we must have conscious access to the complete range of archetypal experiences, and most importantly, the emotions. We must be able to say, yes, I have felt that too; yes, that is part of me. This is the basis for authentic compassion and opening of the heart. This is the purpose of art concerned with the shadow – to remind us these parts of ourselves exist and must be attended to; to bring us, through forceful dramatic presentation, to the revelation of the universal within us.

As we recognize within and accept all possible archetypal experiences, we become integrated. We are no longer split, carrying the emotional pain that results from the rejection of important feeling parts of ourselves. When integration occurs, we experience an unexpected step in personal emotional growth. We transcend the issue and feelings in question. We are no longer held back by the blocking that is always present when feelings are not fully recognized. In unblocking ourselves, we realize our higher potential for relationship, love, and creativity. The road to personal growth lies through the integration of all aspects of human experience.

PANTS

Russell sees an ad in the paper for an "art finishing machine." Curious, he calls to find out more. He is told technology has advanced to the point where it is possible to submit a rough drawing to a computer-based device that will execute a completed, sophisticated, personal work of art in various media based on the input and the personality of the artist. It is able to apply a style and extrapolate the raw data to result in a finished work beyond what the original sketch included, but what it would seem the artist intended.

Russell goes downtown, below Canal Street, to a loft where the company is housed. He is greeted by a representative of the company who shows him around and tells him more about the process. The computer has logged within it technical analysis of all the major styles of the visual arts, both painting and sculpture, which it uses to create its product. For example, when generating a painting, the computer will accept general suggestions about format, but then synthesizes a style, layout, and brushwork pattern based on its knowledge of other art. It directs an apparatus that applies paint to canvas, so a completely realistic result is obtained. Before the painting is executed, it may be viewed on-screen and variables may be adjusted, such as color depth and combination, spontaneity in the strokes, size of brush, etc. Russell is told by the representative, however, that they have learned to not question the wisdom of the computer – they have found it is always right.

He is told it is able to do this not only because of its complex technical knowledge of art, but also because of its familiarity with the emotional state of the artist when the original sketch was made, which it determines through astrology. By using the artist's birth chart and the time of the sketch, it can ascertain, through knowledge of progressions and transits to the chart, and in particular using the moon for exact timing, the precise feelings behind the impulse manifested in the sketch, and can interweave these in the final result, in both content and style. Russell is impressed by all this and takes out a few sketches he has brought with him.

The machine scans his sketches and in minutes is making a succession of paintings. Russell immediately feels a deep connection to the new images – he is fascinated and, in his excitement, even finds himself becoming possessive of the art. His first sketch, a sparse round face with distorted features, has come out of the machine as an abstract expressionistic composition, somewhere between Modigliani and Klee, but the style is new, not an imitation. Russell studies the form, the colors, the mood of the work. He is shocked, seeing not only his character but his feelings behind this particular sketch effortlessly and vividly portrayed in stunning, compelling esthetic excellence.

He studies other paintings, with a similar reaction. He is overwhelmed by the lucidity of the finished work, with how clearly it expresses what he couldn't quite get at on his own, with how he is being presented with a view of himself unknown to him. His ego is dissolved in the presence of the work; he is humbled, he stands naked to himself, no longer with personal will to achieve since there is no longer any purpose in achieving. He becomes aware of how central the need to contact himself was. He breaks down with a rush of emotion and tears in spite of trying to restrain himself because of the representative standing next to him.

After Russell calms down, the representative shows him an idea for a conceptual art series the computer has produced based on another of his sketches. This time, it has recommended a different media, a type of stiff foam plastic. This little-used sculptural material has been chosen especially to make an impression in the current art market, the representative tells him – canvas is no longer in vogue. The idea the computer has come up with using this media is to portray, life-size, pants. The idea occurred to the computer from its analysis of a small part of a rough sketch it juxtaposed with Russell's emotional state at the time of execution.

At that time, Russell was feeling bound down by too much cerebral thinking about his life. He was unable to contact both his free spirit and his groundedness with the natural earth. His sketch reflected this as it subtly highlighted the pants of a certain figure, emphasizing lower body and legs – the part of Russell's physical self that metaphorically needed to be activated to connect him to the earth as well as provide the means for him to walk as an important symbolic prelude for moving from cerebralism to dynamism, and was the means for him to get out of his stuck condition. All of this was, of course, unconscious to Russell.

The computer went on to explain in its discussion of the idea that Russell would not be expressing his "bound-downedness," but the symbolic means to its release and resolution in the depiction of pants. The energetic he would be transferring to the sculptural objects would be entirely positive; viewers of the art would be impacted by this uplifting energy on an unconscious level, and would respond favorably to the works without knowing why. The display of a series of pants on a gallery wall would also be highly enigmatic and evocative in contemporary art circles. Russell decided to make the sculptures, by allowing the computer to fabricate a series of sixteen pants, all with the same energetic, but with varying styles of clothing.

In the gallery, the pants look quite striking. Each life-size pair hangs on a hook at eye level on the gallery wall, with the whole series placed around on four walls with perhaps six feet between each, with stark white background and strong, dramatic lighting. The viewer is, first of all, not sure what material they are made from – they appear completely real. When it is learned they are indeed rigid fabricated and painted sculptures and not simply actual clothing, the viewer is delighted and tantalized by the deception.

Then, attention is drawn to the remarkable detail the computer-driven machinery has been able to achieve in the fabrication. Each pair hangs casually from its hook with complex, natural-looking folds. Each looks as if it is made from its own type of cloth and has its own distinctive belt, also fabricated. Each is worn-out to a different degree. A pair of jeans is torn and well-used, while some elegant formal apparel has no blemishes, and looks hung-up carefree after a memorable night. One pair looks as if they belong to a punk rocker, another to a midwest businessman. A few pair look as if they could be women's slacks, one military. Each pair reflects a distinct type. The collection reaches to another, unforeseen level of significance, documenting and highlighting the diversity of society but also showing the farther-reaching commonality underlying – we all wear pants; we all heed without question society's dictate to cover up; we all shield ourselves and express our identity through our apparel whether we want to or not.

Russell has felt himself completely fulfilled by the art, both inwardly and on an outer-recognition level. In putting his most private self on display, but in obscure form that does not reveal, he has completely made conscious to himself the pattern holding him down. He has completed this cycle of growth, integrating his sense of being bound-down with his untapped potential for inner movement and development. The works have also achieved the intended effect with the audience, delighting and uplifting viewers without their really knowing why, as well as encouraging them to each contact the important hidden resources within.

As he looks back upon his incredible and often doubted liaison with the art computer, Russell smiles to himself. He has relinquished the need to judge; he finds himself not in opposition to the future, but in sync with it. He walks in satisfaction.

About John Ruskan, the artist

John has been on the artist's path all of his life. Working primarily in the music field, he has composed and recorded over 10 albums throughout the years, and continues to release new work. He feels that working as an artist has been a critical factor in his personal growth, especially regarding the cultivation of his right-brain, emotional side.

He was the owner/engineer of Crossfire Recording, one of the first multi-track 'budget' recording studios in New York City in the artistically vibrant 1980's, which hosted a great number of spirited independent recording projects, including his own independent releases on his 22 Records label. He started out as a singer-songwriter, playing guitar and performing solo in public. As electronic music synthesizers became available, he was strongly attracted to the uniqueness of their sound, and started producing compositions ranging from abstract, free-form music to pop song-based pieces.

One of John's guiding artistic principles was always to bring together seemingly opposite forms into a new, hybrid expression. Thus, the singer-songwriter merged with the electronic and resulted in New Wave Rock. Another life-long passion has always been consciousness and Yoga. This merged with the music and produced meditative, instrumental albums unique in the New Age music field, aimed at evoking the deep subconscious along with the transcendental witness.

Throughout, John has been completely comfortable playing all the parts of any musical composition, which was possible because of technological breakthroughs in multi-track recording and synthesizers. He has come to feel more like a painter than a musician, composing and executing the entire musical landscape, and this natural solo artist inclination has enabled him to more easily use his art as a tool for consciousness work, as he has written about here.

In recent years, the trip-hop genre, which is in itself the coming together of two musically opposed fields - catchy rap rhythms and spacey ethereal sounds - has attracted him and resulted in another prolific musical phase.

Although the concept of each of John's albums differs, a common element in his music is the strong 'body' sense. The rhythms are deep and moving, with a deliberant restraint. His intention is to connect to the subconscious through the body, bypassing the mind, evoking and integrating primal and hidden feelings, both in himself and the listener.

In recent years, John's main career focus has been in the psychology field, turning his life-long avocation in consciousness work into a vocation, and re-inventing himself as a writer. A companion book to this present one, called *Emotion and Art*, explores how art can be used as a pathway into the subconscious for healing and growth.

His previous book, which brought together yet another set of opposites, East and West psychology, with a new original synthesis called *Emotional Clearing*, has been widely hailed by experts. His music and other writing is available at **www.johnruskan.com**. His ongoing *Emotional Clearing* work is at **www.emclear.com**.

CPSIA information can be obtained at www.ICGtesting.com
Printed in the USA
LVOW06s1918180214

374219LV00002B/408/P